Joey closed his eyes and shook his head before continuing with his ghost story. "Only one of them returned—covered with blood, shaking hysterically. His hands had been chopped off, and he kept saying over and over, 'Crazy Freddy, Crazy Freddy, Crazy Freddy. . . .' To this day, they are the only words he speaks."

Joey's voice took on a warning tone. "Every once in a while, you can still hear the sound of someone chopping wood deep in the forest late at night. Be very careful. It's no ghost, believe me. It's Crazy Freddy."

The crowd was silent, the flames of the campfire casting eerie shadows on everyone's face. Nicole smiled as she saw Elizabeth shudder. *I think the time has come for the wonder twin to meet Crazy Freddy,* Nicole thought. *One on one.*

CAMP
KILLER

Written by
Kate William

Created by
FRANCINE PASCAL

BANTAM BOOKS
NEW YORK · TORONTO · LONDON · SYDNEY · AUCKLAND

RL 6, age 12 and up

CAMP KILLER

A Bantam Book / July 1996

Sweet Valley High® *is a registered trademark of Francine Pascal*
Conceived by Francine Pascal
Produced by Daniel Weiss Associates, Inc.
33 West 17th Street
New York, NY 10011
Cover art by Bruce Emmett

ISBN: 0-553-56762-4

Published simultaneously in the United States and Canada

Bantam Books are published by Bantam Books, a division of Bantam
Doubleday Dell Publishing Group, Inc. Its trademark, consisting of the
words "Bantam Books" and the portrayal of a rooster, is Registered in U.S.
Patent and Trademark Office and in other countries. Marca Registrada.
Bantam Books, 1540 Broadway, New York, New York 10036.

PRINTED IN THE UNITED STATES OF AMERICA

OPM   0 9 8 7 6 5 4 3 2 1

To Anita Elliot Kaller

Chapter 1

Elizabeth Wakefield closed her eyes as Joey Mason pulled her into his arms for a long, passionate kiss. The nighttime sounds of the forest surrounded them, and a soft, pine-scented breeze ruffled through Elizabeth's long blond hair.

"I wish this night could go on forever," Joey whispered, leaning back against the side of the boathouse.

Elizabeth sighed and rested her head on his shoulder. She and Joey had just returned from a romantic midnight canoe ride on Camp Echo Mountain's Lake Vermillion. An infinite number of stars twinkled in the sky, and a bright crescent moon cast a shimmering silver glow over the lake. It was as if they were in their own special, magical world. Being with Joey seemed so right.

1

But it's not right, a small voice inside her said. Hundreds of miles away, at a basketball camp in Los Angeles, her longtime boyfriend, Todd Wilkins, believed she was being faithful. Elizabeth wrapped her arms more tightly around Joey's strong back and pushed aside the thought.

"Now that we're together again, I never want to let you go," Joey whispered.

"I know," she murmured. "These past few days have been horrible, seeing you and Nicole together—"

Joey stopped her words with a soft kiss. "A new beginning, Elizabeth. From this moment on, let's agree to start over and make the most of the time we have."

She gazed lovingly into his emerald green eyes and nodded. Nicole Banes, a junior counselor from New York, had already tried to ruin enough of Elizabeth's life over the past few weeks. *I won't let her spoil my time with Joey tonight*, Elizabeth vowed.

"You're so special to me," Joey whispered as he ran his fingers through her long blond hair. Elizabeth usually wore it tied back in a ponytail or neatly braided, but in her rush to sneak out of the cabin to meet Joey that night, she hadn't bothered fussing with it. Now, seeing the look of admiration in his eyes, she was glad she hadn't.

A lot more than your hairstyle has changed, the annoying inner voice taunted. This time Elizabeth had more trouble blocking it out, even with the help of Joey's kisses.

At first, spending a month as a junior counselor at a performing-arts camp in Montana had seemed like a great idea. Her identical twin, Jessica, and some of their friends from Sweet Valley High had also signed on to work at Camp Echo Mountain, which was well known for its excellent theater workshops. Elizabeth had always gotten along well with children, and as an aspiring writer, she'd had a keen interest in writing the camp play. *Well, I've accomplished that much,* Elizabeth thought, snuggling closer to Joey.

Joey was the senior counselor in charge of the camp's drama department. Under his direction, Elizabeth's play had come to life earlier that evening. But nothing else at camp had worked out as she'd expected. To get her play produced, she'd had to win the camp's writing contest, and she had raced to get her play finished first. Writing frantically at all hours of the night had left her tired and spacy during the day. The ten-year-old girls she was in charge of had given her the hated nickname of Dizzy Lizzie—and it had stuck.

When Elizabeth had finally finished writing *Lakeside Love,* her play recounting the camp's legend of a woodsman's tragic romance with a camp counselor, Nicole had tried to steal it and pass it off

3

as her own work. Elizabeth shuddered, thinking of how close Nicole had come to getting away with the devious trick.

"Are you cold?" Joey asked softly. His warm breath tickled Elizabeth's ear.

Elizabeth pushed Nicole out of her mind. "What would you do for me if I was?" she challenged in a flirtatious tone.

Joey cocked his head, as if thinking it over carefully. "I'd give you the shirt off my back."

Elizabeth laughed softly, running her lips softly against his. "You're too kind," she teased.

He looked down at his dark blue Yale University sweatshirt. "You're right."

She laughed and shoved him playfully.

He gathered her back into his arms. "Hey, my grandmother gave this sweatshirt to me for my eighteenth birthday last month. I'm only wearing it over the summer so it won't look brand-new when I start school in the fall."

"Sounds like a good plan," Elizabeth joked. "I wouldn't dream of taking such an *important* shirt off your back."

Joey chuckled and then kissed her neck, her chin, her eyes. Elizabeth felt as if she were floating higher than the summit of Echo Mountain, the huge peak that loomed over the camp and the lake.

"OK, it's yours," he said suddenly.

4

Elizabeth opened her eyes to see him shrugging off the sweatshirt. Underneath it he was wearing a black T-shirt with short sleeves. "No, really, Joey, I'm fine," she protested.

"Your arms are covered with goose bumps," he said, slipping his shirt over her head.

"It's way too big," she said, laughing. "But it's so nice and warm. You may never get it back," she told him playfully as she rolled up the sleeves to her wrists.

He cupped her chin in his hands. "I'm sure Yale has other sweatshirts just like it, but you're one of a kind."

Elizabeth felt a rush of pleasure. She knew he was referring to more than just her looks. After all, her looks weren't unique at all; her twin shared the same long blond hair, blue-green eyes, and slim, athletic figure. They even had matching dimples in their left cheeks. Although she and Jessica had very different personalities—Elizabeth was the older, more serious twin, and Jessica was the wild, live-for-the-moment twin—they could pass for each other in appearance. They'd proved it earlier that evening.

As she remembered the events of that day, Elizabeth's hand clenched in a tight fist. "I still can't believe Jessica ditched the play tonight," she seethed. "Sometimes I'd like to stick a homing device in her ear, like they do to keep track of endangered species."

Jessica was supposed to have played the leading female role in *Lakeside Love,* but she'd sneaked away from camp to see a guy she'd recently met. When she hadn't returned in time, Elizabeth had stepped in to cover for her, acting the part she'd written herself. Elizabeth had managed to fool everyone—except Joey.

After the play he had pulled her aside and told her how he felt about her, how much he cared. For the past few days he'd been hanging around Nicole in an attempt to make Elizabeth jealous, and for that he'd apologized.

Joey wrapped his hands around Elizabeth's fist, gently kneading her wrist with his thumbs. "You were fantastic," he said. "You have so much talent and emotional depth."

"I can't believe you knew it was me on that stage tonight," she whispered.

"You're a great actress, but like I said, you're one of a kind." His lips grazed the side of her neck.

A sigh of pleasure escaped her. Joey made her feel so alive, so excited . . . . *and so guilty!* the nasty voice in her head whispered.

Nicole had blackmailed her into breaking up with Joey by threatening to tell Todd about him. At first Elizabeth had given in to Nicole's treachery, but when Joey had kissed her after the play, Elizabeth knew she couldn't stay away from him. *But I sure wish my guilty conscience would shut up once in a while!* she thought.

Elizabeth was suddenly filled with an eerie sense of foreboding. She tried to shake it, but like a dark, sinister force, the woods seemed to be pushing in on her, threatening to engulf her. A branch snapped nearby, and she jumped.

"It's just the wind," Joey said, tightening his arms around her. "Elizabeth, you're shaking."

"I know," she whispered, still terrified. "I think I've heard too many ghost stories around the campfire."

He chuckled. "You want me to walk you to your cabin?"

She shook her head. "Thanks, but the last thing we need is to get caught. I'm already in enough trouble." Lacey Cavannah, the southern widow who owned and operated the camp, set a strict code of behavior for everyone at Camp Echo Mountain. Sneaking out for late-night dates was strictly forbidden. "I think I've already violated at least a dozen camp rules today," Elizabeth said.

"Me, too." Joey brushed a kiss across her forehead and sighed. "I guess we should stash this canoe in the boathouse and get back to our cabins."

Elizabeth reluctantly agreed. Taking care to make as little noise as possible, they carried the canoe into the boathouse. Joey latched the door shut, then reached for her again. "Good night," he whispered.

She leaned forward and kissed him. "Good night."

He gently ran his fingers over her lips. "Sweet dreams, Elizabeth. I know *I'll* be having them— because I'll be dreaming of you." With one last kiss, they parted ways to return to their cabins.

Elizabeth chose not to use her flashlight, fearing the light would give her away. As she hurried along the dark, wooded path to her cabin, her uneasy feeling grew stronger. She replayed Joey's tender parting words in her mind to keep herself from thinking of the dangers that might be lurking in the night.

Something fluttered in the tree above her. Elizabeth's whole body froze. Reluctantly she looked up—and saw a cluster of bats take off into the night sky. Trembling, she hugged Joey's sweatshirt more tightly around her and forced her feet to keep moving. *I guess I'm not cut out for all this sneaking around, the way Jessica is,* she thought wryly.

The rustic cabin that she shared with five other female JCs looked as ominous and spooky as the shadowy woods surrounding it. The faded white-and-red flowery curtains hung limply in the windows, like

8

spirits hovering in the moonlight. The door creaked on its hinges as she pushed it open and stepped inside. Her gaze went immediately to Jessica's bunk, which was empty. The smooth covers seemed to taunt Elizabeth, reminding her of all the dangers that might be lurking in the dark, creepy forest.

A feeling of panic rose in her gut as she tiptoed across the room to her own bunk. It was past midnight, and her sister should have been back hours earlier.

Jessica had originally declared a moratorium on boys and dating for the summer. After the recent death of her boyfriend Christian Gorman, she'd sworn off getting involved with anyone else. Instead, she'd dived right into camp life, endearing herself to everyone from campers to counselors. The seven- and eight-year-old girls in her group adored her and followed her constantly, copying her every move. Jessica had nicknamed them the Wanna-bes. Even Lacey had gone out of her way to praise Jessica's leadership and maturity.

But then Jessica had fallen for Paul Mathis, the older brother of one of her Wanna-bes, who lived in a nearby town. That evening, reverting to her former reckless self, she'd pedaled to town on an old camp bicycle to see him, leaving Elizabeth to pick up the pieces.

Across the room, Jessica's best friend, Lila

Fowler, lay softly snoring, her body tangled among real linen sheets and a silk-covered down comforter. Lila came from one of the wealthiest families in Sweet Valley and freely applied her family's money to smooth out as much of the "roughing it" aspect of camping as she could—including sending away for new, luxurious bedding to replace the worn cotton and wool provided by the camp.

Elizabeth crept across the room and stood over Lila's sleeping form. "Wake up!" she whispered urgently, shaking Lila's shoulder.

Lila rolled over and groaned, her light brown hair falling over her face. "I wanna see . . . gardens . . ."

Elizabeth shook her again, harder. "Wake up. Jessica isn't back yet. We have to go find her."

"Go away," Lila mumbled.

"Wake up, Lila! It's an emergency."

Lila's eyes opened, gleaming like two brown daggers. "Thanks a lot. You just killed the most beautiful dream." She yawned, ending it on a deep sigh. "I was in Paris. Bo and I were walking along the Champs-Elysées, the most beautiful street in the world. . . . Springtime is just gorgeous in Paris." She closed her eyes, smiling, trying to recapture the image of Bo, the wealthy JC from Washington, D.C., who she met that summer.

"Come on!" Elizabeth said, shaking her again. "I'm worried sick about Jessica."

"Bug off," Lila grumbled, pressing her face into her pillow. An instant later she bolted upright, suddenly alert, her eyes alive with curiosity. "Where have *you* been?" she asked. "If I didn't know better, I'd think I was dreaming right now. Imagine Elizabeth Wakefield sneaking out in the middle of the night." She folded her arms and grinned knowingly. "My intuition tells me there has to be a guy in this somewhere."

Elizabeth sighed wearily. "Not now, Lila."

"OK, let me guess." Lila scooted over and patted the vacant spot, gesturing for Elizabeth to sit. "Was it . . . Joey Mason?"

"Oh, all right," Elizabeth said, relenting. She sat on the edge of the bed. She knew Lila was stubborn enough to badger her all night until her thirst for gossip was satisfied. "Yes, I was with Joey," Elizabeth admitted. "We went for a canoe ride. Big deal."

Lila raised her eyebrows. "A canoe ride in the moonlight . . . sounds romantic. And I do believe that's his sweatshirt you're wearing. Does this mean you're through with Todd?"

"No, of course not," Elizabeth replied adamantly. "I love Todd. He and I are . . . never mind, Lila. You wouldn't understand." *I don't understand it, either,* her guilty conscience added.

Lila shrugged. "What's there to understand? It

11

seems pretty simple to me. I guess the Wakefield twins are more identical than we thought."

"Very funny," Elizabeth shot back. "Are you going to help me find Jessica or not?"

"Not." Lila lay back down and snuggled under the covers. "Go to bed, Elizabeth. Jessica can take care of herself. She's probably having a great time."

Elizabeth watched in frustration as Lila yawned and closed her eyes. *Now what?* she wondered. She couldn't go out looking for Jessica by herself, and she was too worried to go to sleep.

She returned to her own bed and sat on top of the covers, determined to wait up for her twin. At times like these, she felt as if she were more than four minutes older than Jessica. Taking care of her younger sister was a full-time responsibility.

In the bed next to hers, Maria Slater rolled over and mumbled something incoherent. The moonlight picked up the color of her rich ebony complexion and near-perfect facial features.

Elizabeth unlaced her hiking boots and pulled them off her feet. Taking care not to drop them, she placed them on the floor next to her bed.

She'd been thrilled when she'd learned that Maria, an old friend whom she hadn't seen for years, would also be at Camp Echo Mountain. Maria had moved to Sweet Valley during sixth grade. Her charming, outgoing personality had made her an instant success with the kids at Sweet Valley Middle School. When everyone had learned that Maria had been a famous child actress, she'd become even more popular—especially with Jessica.

But Elizabeth's friendship with Maria had begun with their shared commitment to writing. Elizabeth had felt as if she could talk to Maria about anything.

A few years later, Maria's mother had taken a job with a New York City record company, and the Slater family had moved to the East Coast. Elizabeth could still remember how sad she'd been to lose her good friend.

Elizabeth leaned back against the wall and sighed wearily. The week before camp started, Maria had surprised her with a phone call and great news. Not only would they be together at camp, but Maria's family was planning to move back to Sweet Valley in the fall. Then Maria had mentioned that her best friend from New York would also be at camp. . . .

Elizabeth could still hear Maria's excited words gushing over the line: *You two have so much in common, I'm sure you'll get along just great!*

Maria's friend turned out to be one of the most hateful girls Elizabeth had ever met—Nicole Banes. *The bane of my existence!* she thought wryly.

Elizabeth pulled her knees up to her chin and

wrapped her arms around her legs. Since the moment they'd first come in contact with each other, she and Nicole had clashed. Their first battle had been over the old, scarred wooden desk in the cabin. Soon other prizes had been thrown into the arena—Maria's friendship, the respect of their fellow counselors, the camp play, and of course Joey.

Elizabeth tucked her arms under Joey's sweatshirt, snuggling in its comforting warmth. *I can't wait to see what Nicole thinks of my new Yale sweatshirt,* Elizabeth mused, remembering the time Nicole had returned from a date with Joey wearing his T-shirt. Nicole had slept in it, then carried on all morning about the wonderful time they'd had.

You won't be gloating now, Elizabeth told Nicole in her head. It was a small but satisfying victory.

Across the room, Nicole lay peacefully on her side, perfectly still except for the rise and fall of her chest as she breathed slowly and rhythmically. Her conscience didn't seem to bother her at all. She looked like an innocent child, with her arms curled around her pillow as if she were holding a favorite doll. The dark red baseball cap she always wore backward on her head was on the nightstand next to her bed.

You can't tell what a person's like by her looks, Elizabeth reminded herself. *You of all people should know that.* Beneath Nicole's wholesome good looks and sporty, upbeat style, the girl was pure snake.

Elizabeth shifted nervously. She was certain that it would be only a matter of time before Nicole struck again. Being a junior counselor was exhausting enough without having to guard her back constantly against a sneak attack. Plus she was carrying a heavy load of guilt for cheating on Todd—and now she was losing sleep over Jessica. *How long can I go on like this,* she wondered, *before I go completely nuts?*

I love Todd . . . I'm worried sick about Jessica. Lying in her bed, pretending to be asleep, Nicole mentally mocked Elizabeth's pathetic whining. *What a big show-off!* Nicole couldn't stand the fake worry in Elizabeth's voice.

Elizabeth Wakefield deserved to be punished for all the things she'd stolen from her—Joey, Maria, and the play. Nicole was the one who should have been taking the bows for writing *Lakeside Love.* And Maria was her best friend in the whole world. Elizabeth had no right to move in and steal her away.

But the real kicker was Joey. She'd met him

three years before, when she'd first started coming to Camp Echo Mountain. Joey had been a junior counselor back then, and as a camper, Nicole hadn't stood a chance; dating between counselors and campers was strictly forbidden. She'd waited so long for this, her first summer as junior counselor, because it meant that she and Joey could finally get together. Or so she'd thought. Until Elizabeth-the-wonder-twin Wakefield had come along and shattered her dreams.

Nicole's jaw clenched. She wasn't beaten yet, not by a long shot. Dizzy Lizzie was going to be very sorry for what she'd done. Nicole ducked her head under the covers and laughed softly. Revenge was so much fun. *Get ready, Dizzy Lizzie,* Nicole thought cheerfully as she drifted off to sleep. *It's payback time.*

Chapter 2

With only a flashlight to penetrate the dark, Jessica Wakefield followed Paul Mathis down a deserted country road. "We must've walked at *least* ten miles already," she complained.

Paul turned to her and smiled. He was devastatingly gorgeous, with wavy black hair and muscular shoulders—and well worth any punishment Lacey Cavannah might throw at Jessica for sneaking away from camp. Except, of course, being sent home. That was the one threat that kept Jessica focused on getting back to camp.

"Come on, Jessica, don't wimp out on me now," Paul teased.

She raised her chin defiantly and glared at him. "I don't 'wimp out'—ever. Besides, if I were a wimp, would I be here with you now, wandering around in the dark in the middle of nowhere?"

He pulled her into his arms and kissed her. "We aren't wandering around," he said, his dark eyes twinkling with amusement. "I know exactly where we're going."

"Yeah, right. You said you had a plan to get me back to camp, but if it's so great, why won't you tell me what it is?"

"Trust me," he said.

Jessica gave him a crooked smile. "Seems I don't have much of a choice, do I?"

Paul chuckled softly and tucked a lock of her long blond hair behind her ear. "Nope. You're all mine tonight."

His words sent an unexpected thrill up and down her spine. Standing on tiptoe, she reached up and kissed him, then playfully shoved him onward. "OK, let's see this brilliant plan of yours before Lacey discovers I'm gone and kicks me out of Camp Echo Mountain for good."

Paul entwined his fingers with hers and brought her hand up to his lips. "I won't let that happen," he said.

Jessica sighed. Her hand felt so right in his. After Christian died, she'd assumed she'd be alone for a long time. It was as if something inside her had died with him and she'd never be able to love again. So when she'd first arrived at Camp Echo

Mountain, she had planned on having a no-boys summer.

Giving up the roller-coaster ride of falling in love, she'd been content to stand back and watch as Elizabeth tortured herself over Joey Mason and Lila made a fool of herself over Bo. The no-boys plan had worked like a charm, keeping Jessica's heart safe—until Paul had come to camp to pick up his little sister, Tanya. With one look into Paul's dark, sexy eyes, Jessica's resolve had melted away like ice in the desert.

Jessica looked up at the huge expanse of stars in the night sky. Thanks to Paul, her heart had healed. And once again the wild, fun-loving Jessica Wakefield was back in full force. The downside was that she'd lost her good standing with Lacey, but that couldn't be helped. The camp rules that kept Jessica and Paul apart had to be broken. It was as simple as that.

"Can you at least give me a hint?" Jessica asked.

"Think of it as a surprise," he said.

"This had better be good, Paul. I'm already on Lacey's last-chance list." The week before, Jessica had "borrowed" Lacey's Ford Bronco to drive into town to see Paul. Unfortunately, Lacey had hinted that she was aware of Jessica's late-night drives, forcing Jessica to come up with a different means of transportation.

That evening she'd pedaled into town on an old camp bicycle. It had been a long, strenuous ride. If she hadn't been in such good shape from cheerleading and surfing, she'd never have made it.

When she had arrived at *Matties*, the restaurant Paul's parents owned, he'd already gone home. One of the waiters had offered her a ride to Paul's house, so Jessica had left the bike at the restaurant. Hours later, after a wonderful time with Paul, she'd found herself stranded at his house, which was miles from town and even farther from camp. She hoped Elizabeth had been able to cover for her in the camp play without being caught—otherwise Jessica's summer in Montana might come to an abrupt end.

The wind whistled through the trees, sending a wave of pine fragrance into the cool night air. From somewhere in the darkness, a low, guttural moan startled her. "What was that?" she shrieked.

Paul laughed. "It was a cow, Jessica. We have a lot of them in Montana."

"Oh," Jessica said with a shrug. An instant later, she started laughing, too.

Paul slipped his arm around her shoulders and hugged her to his side. "You seem jumpy tonight," he said.

"It's probably all the ghost stories they tell at camp. Lacey told us about a woodsman who used to work at the camp years ago. He was fired when they discovered he'd been fooling around with the head counselor. A few days later, the two of them disappeared, leaving all their stuff behind. No one ever saw them again. But sometimes, late at night, you can still hear the sound of the woodsman's ghost chopping wood deep in the forest." Jessica stopped and turned to him. "Isn't that weird?"

"Yeah," he said, feigning a serious tone. "And you think they're hiding in the dark, impersonating cows?"

She punched his arm. "Would you forget about the cow? It just startled me, that's all. Anyway, Elizabeth used the story in her play. I was supposed to play the part of Cassandra, the heartbroken head counselor who chooses to give up her whole life to follow her banished lover into the woods. Then, realizing their love is doomed, they eat poison berries and die in each other's arms."

Jessica swooned dramatically. It had been a great role, and she was disappointed that she'd missed the play—especially considering how hard she'd rehearsed over the past few days. *But it was worth it to be with Paul,* she reminded herself.

Paul whistled as if he was amazed. "I have to warn you, Jessica. There is a chance that Lacey will catch me tonight and banish me from Camp Echo Mountain. I hope you're not planning to eat poison berries if that happens."

Jessica punched his arm, laughing. "You're pushing it, Paul."

After they'd walked a bit longer, he shone his flashlight on a low barbed wire fence. "We have to climb over this," he said softly.

Several dark, shadowy buildings loomed just up ahead. Jessica frowned. "Where are we?"

He touched his finger to his lips, gesturing for silence. "It's a surprise, remember?"

With an exaggerated sigh, Jessica followed him over the fence. "We have to kill the lights now," he whispered. "Watch where you step."

"Great," she grumbled sarcastically as Paul led her to one of the buildings. "Can you tell me now?" she asked.

"This is my neighbor's horse barn," he answered proudly.

"What are we—" Her question hung in the air as she watched him open the double doors. "I don't know about this, Paul," she said with a giggle as she followed him inside.

The barn smelled of hay and horse manure. Paul turned on the light, a bare lightbulb with a short pull chain mounted on the wall, and led Jessica by the hand to the first of several stalls. A reddish brown horse with huge dark eyes stared at her. "Meet Phil," Paul said with a proud smile.

"A horse?" Jessica shrieked. "*This* is your brilliant

plan—stealing a horse? Don't they hang people around here for stealing horses?"

He winced. "'Stealing' is such a harsh word. I like to think of this as . . . taking my old pal Phil out for some healthy exercise. Besides," he added, his eyes twinkling with contained laughter, "I don't think a car thief has any right to act so high and mighty all of a sudden."

Jessica raised her eyebrows and glared at him. "I did not steal Lacey's car. I *borrowed* it."

"And now you've graduated to 'borrowing' horses. I'll have to keep an eye on you, Jessica. Next thing we know, you'll be 'borrowing' cash from First Bank of Montana."

"Very funny, Paul. And to think you were such a grouch when I first met you." He'd had his reasons, as Jessica had learned. A relationship he'd had with a former JC had left him heartbroken and wary of trying again.

He laughed and kissed her swiftly. "I guess I just couldn't resist your brand of magic."

A warm glow surrounded her as she watched Paul deftly saddle up the horse. "It's not going to be a fast ride," he said, leading Phil out of the stall, "but at least you'll be back at camp by morning."

"I'd better be," she said.

Paul hopped into the saddle and reached his hand down to help Jessica. She settled in behind him and wrapped her arms around his waist.

"You all right back there?" he asked over his shoulder.

Jessica leaned forward and snuggled against his lean, broad back. "This isn't so bad," she murmured. A minute later, when Phil broke into a steady gallop, she decided it was terrific. The wind was in her hair, and she was riding though the moonlit night on horseback with her arms around a gorgeous guy. *What could be more romantic?* she thought.

She was running through the black woods, her heart pumping as if it were ready to explode. The path disappeared . . . something crashed . . .

Elizabeth awoke with a start, a soundless scream lodged in her throat. Afraid to move anything but her eyes, she studied her shadowy surroundings. An ugly knot in the plywood ceiling above her head seemed to have taken the form of a grotesque, leering face. For a moment she didn't know where she was.

A nightmare, she realized, sighing with relief. Something had been chasing her, but she couldn't remember the details. She sat up, moaning at the stiffness in her muscles. Her neck was especially sore, having been bent at an odd angle while she slept.

24

Elizabeth rubbed her eyes and noticed she was still fully dressed, sitting on top of the covers. Then she remembered why—*Jessica*. She glanced over at her twin's bed, which was still empty.

Elizabeth grabbed her flashlight and wristwatch from her nightstand and ducked under the covers to check the time. "Three-fifteen!" she whispered. *Jessica, where are you?* her mind screamed. The eerie silence of the night made Elizabeth's skin crawl. She was sure there was something wicked brewing out there. She wrapped her arms around her knees, grateful for the soothing comfort of Joey's warm sweatshirt, and closed her eyes.

Suddenly Elizabeth heard a crash outside the cabin, the same sound she'd heard in her dream. Her eyes flew open, and her heart jumped to her throat.

The door opened, and Jessica tiptoed into the cabin. Flooded with anger as well as tremendous relief, Elizabeth jumped out of bed. "Where have you been?" she hissed.

Jessica giggled. Elizabeth's bossy, big-sister attitude was completely wasted on her. Still glowing from her fabulous time with Paul, Jessica crept over to her sister's bed and plopped down on the mattress. "Wait till you hear about the night I've had," Jessica whispered dreamily, pulling Elizabeth down by her arm to sit next to her. "I was stranded at Paul's house because his parents had taken his truck. He brought me back on a horse named Phil. It was fabulous. I'm in love."

"With a horse?" Elizabeth said wryly.

Jessica ignored the snide comment. "It was so much fun, Liz. You wouldn't believe how romantic it is to ride a horse through the night. . . ." She sighed with delight just thinking about it.

"I can't believe you left me to act your part in the play," Elizabeth said, her voice indignant. "It was a stupid move, Jessica."

"I know," Jessica agreed with remorse. "I'm sorry about missing my chance to be in your play. I was so excited about it, and I worked so hard getting ready for it." Her daily rehearsals had been squeezed into an already full schedule of teaching dance workshops, looking after her group of seven- and eight-year-old Wanna-bes, and doing her share of camp chores.

But any regret she might have had was wiped away by the joyful memory of her body snuggled against Paul's, the wind whipping through her hair, the way it had felt to laugh. "Seeing Paul was a hundred times more important, Liz. And I knew you could handle playing me for a few hours." She shrugged. "So, did we get caught?" she asked.

"No," Elizabeth admitted.

"See, no harm done," Jessica replied flippantly. "By the way, I see you're wearing Joey's sweatshirt. Seems your night was also a great success." She started to get up, but Elizabeth pulled her back down.

"Please, Jessica, you have to promise me you'll never do something like this again."

Although she'd expected a lecture sooner or later, Jessica was surprised by the urgency in her sister's voice.

"I have this odd feeling," Elizabeth explained. "Something is going on in this camp—something bad."

Jessica waved her hand, dismissing Elizabeth's concerns. "Oh, come on, Liz. I know things haven't been going very well for you, but—"

Elizabeth gripped her arm. "I mean it, Jess. You have to promise me you'll be careful and that you'll never leave camp alone, like you did tonight."

Jessica saw the frantic look on Elizabeth's face and knew it was pointless to argue. "Sure, whatever," she said to appease Elizabeth. But even as Jessica spoke the words she crossed her fingers behind her back—just in case the opportunity for another marvelous, thrilling, romantic adventure with Paul Mathis happened to come along.

"I think I'm getting used to Bernard's cooking," Maria said to Nicole at breakfast the following morning. She plopped herself down at Nicole's table, squeezing in between Nicole and Lara O'Mally, a fifteen-year-old camper in Nicole's group. Lara made a face at Maria and mumbled something rude. Nicole glared at the redheaded girl, letting her know that her behavior wasn't acceptable. Lara's attitude instantly changed, and she went back to talking to her friends. *You have to show these kids who's the boss,* Nicole thought.

"Have you tried the corn muffins?" Maria asked. "They aren't too bad."

"They're probably store-bought," Nicole answered flatly. She didn't care if Bernard, the camp's head cook, made everything taste like poison. Her day had already been ruined. She'd woken up that morning to see Elizabeth stalking around the cabin wearing Joey's Yale sweatshirt. Nicole was still fuming over the smug look the wonder twin had given her.

Anyway, her friendship with Maria was probably all over, thanks to Elizabeth Wakefield and her meddlesome twin sister. One of Jessica's campers, Maggie, an eight-year-old brat with brown pigtails and freckles, had secretly videotaped a conversation in which Nicole had been teasing Elizabeth about having stolen her play. OK, so maybe Nicole had been mean to Elizabeth, but the girl deserved it. Everyone knew Nicole was supposed to have written the camp play.

28

But Jessica had discovered Maggie's tape and played it for the entire camp to see, embarrassing Nicole in front of everyone who mattered. Sure, Maria was still speaking to her, but that was probably because she felt sorry for her. Nicole resented being a charity case. "Don't you think you should go sit with your campers?" Nicole asked in her best haughty-sounding voice.

Maria shrugged. "They're all right for a few minutes." She kept chatting cheerfully, but Nicole wasn't listening. She was distracted by the disgusting sight of Elizabeth fawning over Joey in the food line. It wasn't fair that Dizzy Lizzie had an identical twin to help fight her battles.

As she glared at Elizabeth and Joey, Nicole felt a little of her usual strength springing to life. *I'm not defeated yet,* she thought. *There's no way I'd ever let a sneaky do-gooder like Elizabeth Wakefield get the best of me.* Even with both Wakefield twins ganging up on her, Nicole was determined to win back everything she'd lost.

An all-camp color war was planned for the last Saturday of camp, which was less than two weeks away. Two days before, Lacey had drawn Nicole's and Elizabeth's names as captains of the two opposing teams. *It's as if the wonder twin and I are fated to battle each other,* Nicole mused. Thinking about it made her smile.

If only Joey were on my red team, Nicole thought. She wondered if Lacey had assigned the campers and counselors to teams yet. *I'd sure love to get my hands on that list.*

"You're not listening, are you?" Maria asked.

Nicole put on a sweet, innocent smile. "I was thinking about the color war."

"Are you excited to be a team captain?" Maria asked.

"Oh, yes, I am," she said. "I just hope we win." To herself she added, *I guarantee we'll win. My red team is going to beat Elizabeth's blue team—and Elizabeth's blond head—to a pulp.* She shoveled a forkful of dry, tasteless scrambled eggs into her mouth.

Maria looked at her with a searching expression. "I think you and Elizabeth would get along if you'd just try."

Nicole swallowed and glared at Maria. "Oh, so now it's all my fault?" she said indignantly.

Maria shook her head and sighed. "Forget it. I guess it's a lost cause. But it's really hard on me."

"What about me?" Nicole said. "That girl has—" She saw Maria roll her eyes. "Never mind," Nicole said, feeling stung. She was completely on her own, thanks to the wonder twin. *And for that, she's going to pay—starting right now!*

Nicole stood abruptly and picked up her tray.

Carefully putting on a cheerful expression, she made a show of checking her watch. "Look at the time. Sorry, but I have to go."

"It's still early," Maria said.

"I know." Nicole chewed her bottom lip and glanced nervously at the door. "I have to pick up a few things at the boathouse before my first water-skiing class," she said breezily. "See ya later!"

Chapter 3

Lacey's office was very plain and impeccably organized. *Like Lacey herself,* Nicole thought. A gray file cabinet stood against the wall, behind a wooden desk and leather office chair. Nicole knew the camp routine well enough to know that with breakfast, A.M. cabin checks, and Lacey's morning walk, the place would be deserted.

Nicole pulled open the file drawer labeled Current Season and scanned the straight row of neatly typed labels. There was a file on each of the JCs, and she would have loved to linger over those, especially the one on Elizabeth. *Some other time,* she promised herself as she grabbed the file marked Color War.

She was pleased to see that Maria had been assigned to the red team. Fighting together against

Elizabeth might help to repair their friendship. Unfortunately, Joey's name was on the blue team's list. "We can't have that," she whispered.

Nicole carefully erased Joey's name, then skimmed the red team's list to see whom she was willing to give up to Elizabeth. "Let's see. . . . What about Winston Egbert?"

Winston was an OK guy, funny and entertaining, sort of cute, but not very athletic. He wouldn't be much of a loss, especially since he was from Sweet Valley and a good friend of Elizabeth's.

OK, Dizzy Lizzie, I'll trade you one clown for one hunk, Nicole thought as she carefully penciled in the changes. Feeling quite pleased with herself, she replaced the file and shut the drawer.

For the first time since Jessica Wakefield had publicly humiliated her with Maggie's videotape, Nicole was thrilled to be at Camp Echo Mountain. Rearranging the team lists was only the beginning. *Things are about to get tough for the wonder twin,* Nicole decided. By the end of the color war, Joey would be hers. And Elizabeth would be scared of her own shadow.

As Nicole slipped out of the white house in which Lacey's apartment and the camp offices were located, she was nearly bowled over by a herd of rowdy twelve-year-old boys. "Watch it!" she hollered.

"Hey, Nicole!" one of the boys shouted. "Are

33

you going to be wearing your orange swimsuit today?" he asked, referring to her skimpiest bikini. A few of the others sniggered and hooted.

Aaron Dallas, the JC who'd been leading them to the archery range, swiped the offender's baseball cap and swatted him with it. "You'll have to excuse these animals, Nicole. They've been drinking too much bug juice."

Aaron was from Sweet Valley and not bad-looking. He was also a great athlete. *I should have grabbed him for my team, too,* Nicole thought.

He replaced the kid's cap, then turned to Nicole. "So," he said, grinning, "are you?"

"Am I what?" Nicole asked.

He shrugged, giving her an innocent look. "Are you planning to wear the orange swimsuit?"

Nicole laughed, partly irritated and partly flattered, and swatted him with her own baseball cap. "Get a life, Aaron!"

"Go on, Lila," Bo said. "Tell me more about this dream of yours. What happens after we get to the Jardin des Plantes? I was there two years ago, by the way. It's one of the finest botanical gardens in the world."

Lila giggled, wondering if she should reveal the steamy parts. "Well," she said with a coy smile, "let's just say we got into the Paris spirit of things."

They were strolling hand in hand along the shore of the lake. She was supposed to be in the arts and crafts cabin, helping to teach thirteen-year-olds how to make woven ribbon bags. But Suzanne, the senior counselor in charge of arts and crafts, was capable enough to handle the little brats, so it hardly made sense for Lila to miss out on such a glorious afternoon.

Not that she was the outdoorsy type. Lila's nature-lover experiences were generally limited to sunbathing, driving her Triumph convertible with the top down, and the occasional beach-ball toss. She'd only agreed to come to Camp Echo Mountain out of loyalty to Jessica.

Putting her friend's needs first was unusual for Lila. It wasn't that she didn't care about her friends. But neither she nor Jessica was the warm and fuzzy kind. They were more often than not locked in fierce competition over everything from boys to clothes.

But after Jessica had lost her boyfriend to gang violence, Lila had felt obligated to offer whatever support she could—even to the point of spending an entire month in the backwoods, far from civilization.

The accommodations were depressingly ugly and filthy—they even had to walk to a separate building to go to the bathroom! The place was seriously understaffed; the JCs were expected to do chores such as peeling vegetables and washing dishes. And the food was ghastly. Bernard's culinary skills stopped at cornflakes and bottled orange juice. If it weren't for the express orders she'd faxed to Season's Gourmet Shop in Sweet Valley and the Western Meadowlark air cargo service, which picked up the food packages in Billings and delivered them to camp, Lila and Bo would have starved to death days earlier.

To make things worse, Lila had been saddled with a bunch of thirteen-year-old whiners who considered themselves too old and sophisticated for camp. She called them the Sulky Six. Tiffany was the leader of the group and the most annoying. With her tall, skinny body, long eyelashes, and blond hair, the girl acted as if she were the last word in fashion and glamour. She constantly bragged that when she got her braces off, she was going to be a famous model.

Her best friend, Amber, came in a close second on the obnoxiousness scale. Amber had strawberry blond hair, blue eyes, and flawless, porcelainlike skin. She had a few extra pounds of fat on her, which seemed to keep her from dreaming of a modeling career. But Lila thought Amber was the real beauty of the group.

Nancy and Robin were jock types who resented the fact that they weren't at sports camp. Samantha and Odette were African American fraternal twins from Georgia. Samantha, the beauty of the pair, was spoiled rotten. Odette wasn't too bad, although she was a nerd. She usually kept to herself, reading or watching the others with an amused expression. Lila figured Odette had inherited the extra brain cells that Samantha lacked.

But despite its many drawbacks, Camp Echo Mountain was turning out to be the most thrilling romantic adventure of Lila's life.

Bo stopped walking and took her into his arms. "If you want Paris in springtime, then you should have it."

Her mouth went dry as she gazed into his warm brown eyes. He was her soul mate, and the hottest guy she'd ever known.

Bo, whose full name was Beauregard Creighton III, came from a background of wealth and privilege similar to hers. His father was a self-made million-aire, as hers was. And he hated camping as much as she did. Bo was one of those for whom the term "roughing it" meant having to stay in anything less than a five-star hotel.

When they'd first met, though, they'd both pre-tended to be the hardy, outdoorsy type, each trying to impress the other with made-up stories about their death-defying adventures in the wilderness. But the truth had finally come out, to Lila's relief, and after a good laugh they had realized what a perfect couple they made.

Bo kissed her softly. "How about giving me a chance to create Paris in springtime for you right here?"

"How are you going to do that?" she asked, intrigued.

A glint of laughter shone in his eyes. "It's a surprise. Meet me for dinner tomorrow night in the clearing behind the equipment shed."

"Don't you have kitchen duty tomorrow night?" she asked. The daily roster of JC duty assignments was posted every morning. Lila knew Bo's schedule as well as her own.

"Don't you worry about that, Lila. I've got it covered." He flashed her an utterly sexy, lopsided grin and squeezed her hand. "Tomorrow night, you and me—it'll be great, I promise."

She wrapped her arms around his neck and smiled. "Oh, I'm sure it will be. I just don't know if I can wait."

At lunch the ten-year-old girls in Elizabeth's group went on and on about the fabulous time they'd had in Nicole's waterskiing class that morning. Elizabeth's relationship with the girls had improved with the success of *Lakeside Love,* but they still occasionally called her Diz and often went out of their way to irritate her.

"I can't wait to try the new jump!" Aimee, a sturdy, brown-haired girl, said. She was the leader of the group and the one who had first come up with Dizzy Lizzie.

"Me neither," her friend Helen said. Helen had dark hair and round tortoiseshell glasses that made her eyes seem extra large. She always echoed everything Aimee said.

Emily, a pretty girl with honey blond hair and green eyes, chimed in. "Nicole said everyone has to be able to do the double hold first."

Sitting across from Emily, Ashley flipped her wavy blond hair behind her shoulder and shrugged. "I don't see why. The double hold is a lot harder."

"Nicole's an expert. I'm sure she knows what she's doing," Adrienne said. Adrienne was the radical-looking member of the group, with three silver studs in her left ear and close-cropped brown hair.

The only girl at the table who wasn't part of the conversation was Jennifer, who at that moment was busy transporting strawfuls of milk from her glass to her peanut butter sandwich, soaking the bread, oblivious to the fact that the ends of her red hair were in her vanilla pudding. Elizabeth shuddered. The girl had the worst table manners she'd ever seen.

"Are you going to try that backward hold Nicole

showed us today?" Emily asked the others, her green eyes wide with obvious enthusiasm.

"I am," Aimee said.

Helen nodded. "Me too."

Jennifer accidentally knocked over her glass, splashing a shower of milk on Helen's tortoiseshell glasses and soaking Elizabeth's yellow T-shirt.

"Nice going," Aimee said. Elizabeth shot dirty looks at all of them and rushed to the kitchen for a dishrag.

She was cleaning up the mess when Maria stopped by the table. "How's it going?" Maria asked.

Elizabeth shook her head. "Don't ask."

Maria gave her a sympathetic look. "That bad?"

"Worse," Elizabeth muttered, wringing the wet rag over her tray.

"All heads bow," Maria whispered. "Our fearless leader approaches." Elizabeth looked up as Lacey Cavannah entered the mess hall for mail call, banging a pan with a spoon for attention.

"Her brown fedora is just *so* cool," Maria mumbled sarcastically. "I'd *love* to get a hat just like it."

Elizabeth stifled a laugh.

The room quieted down as Lacey handed out the day's mail in alphabetical order. When Elizabeth's name was called, Lacey handed her a large padded envelope.

Elizabeth carried it back to her seat and set it

on the table next to her tray. Todd's bold handwriting seemed to jump off the label.

Maria looked at her. "Come on, Elizabeth, I'm dying to see what it is."

Aimee leaned over and read the return address. "It's from Diz's boyfriend, Todd. How sweet."

"How sweet," Helen echoed.

Elizabeth glowered at her, then tore open the package. Inside were several items nestled between sheets of old newspaper: a plastic tube of insecticide, which the label proclaimed was made from an "all-natural, secret blend of herbs," a box of light blue stationery embossed with the letter *E,* and a book of old-movie trivia. There was also a letter, which she slipped into the pocket of her shorts.

Maria was watching her with an intense, straightforward expression. "Todd is really nice, Elizabeth. You're very lucky to have such a thoughtful boyfriend." Her tone made it sound like a warning.

Racked with guilt, Elizabeth nodded. She couldn't believe how horribly she was treating him. But then she looked up and saw Joey walking toward her. His warm smile tugged at her heart. Right or wrong, her feelings for him were too strong to deny. Elizabeth gathered up the contents of Todd's care package and stuffed everything back into the envelope.

Maria leaned forward and whispered, "I hope you know what you're doing."

Elizabeth swallowed hard, hoping the same thing, but she just nodded at Maria. Tucking the package under her arm, she looked up and smiled at Joey. "Aren't you going to have lunch?" she asked.

"I wish I could," he said, eyeing her tray with a glint of amusement. "That green stuff looks delicious."

Aimee giggled and pointed to the peas on Elizabeth's tray. They'd been boiled beyond recognition and then burned. "Oh, you mean that? That's where Jennifer threw up."

"I did not!" Jennifer shrieked, picking up a wet strip of bread as if she was going to toss it at Aimee.

Elizabeth grabbed Jennifer's wrist. "Don't even think about it," she warned. *Why do they always seem to pick the worst moments to act like monsters?* she wondered.

She felt humiliated to have Joey see how little control she had over them, but his expression was completely understanding and sympathetic. He winked, and a flush of pleasure rose in Elizabeth's cheeks.

Lacey banged on her pot again. "I have the team lists for the color war," she announced, holding up two sheets of paper. "Will our two team captains please stand?"

A smattering of cheers as well as jeers rang out as Elizabeth rose to her feet. "Nicole is still on the boat," ten-year-old Bryan Parker said. "She's fixing the tow bar because Tad broke it."

"I did not!" Tad Winslow shouted. Tad, one of Bryan's cabinmates, was a round-faced boy with a crew cut.

Lacey blew her whistle and shot the rowdy boys a silencing look. "I'm going to post these lists on the bulletin board outside, along with sign-up sheets for the day's events. Each JC must also volunteer for one setup activity."

As soon as Lacey finished speaking, the room erupted with a buzz of excitement. Weeks before, when she'd first announced the color war, the idea hadn't sparked much enthusiasm among the JCs. Elizabeth had also questioned its value; in her opinion, these campers needed a crash course in cooperation, not competition. Neither did she like the idea of being publicly pitted against Nicole Banes. Still, Elizabeth found herself getting caught up in the excitement of the moment as everyone hurried outside to read the team lists.

Standing right behind Elizabeth in front of the bulletin board, Joey groaned. "I'm on the red team."

Elizabeth felt a pang of disappointment. "So is Maria," she said.

Joey nuzzled the back of her head. "If you try very hard, I bet you can bribe me to divulge team secrets."

"Sounds interesting," she said wistfully. At least Jessica was on the blue team, for which Elizabeth was thankful. She wanted to keep a close watch on her twin.

Chapter 4

Lacey's announcement was just the distraction Jessica needed. While everyone else was milling around the bulletin board outside, she used the phone inside the lodge to call Paul at his parents' restaurant.

After she had spent several frustrating minutes on hold, Paul's voice finally came on the line. Jessica could hardly hear him with all the noise in the background—pots clanging, plates rattling, people yelling food orders.

"Sorry to keep you waiting, Jess," he shouted. "I'm working the grill today, and we're in the middle of the dinner rush."

"Dinner?" she said. "It's still afternoon."

He laughed. "We country folks eat dinner now and supper later. Anyway, what's up?"

"Tomorrow night would be a great time for me to sneak away and meet you," she said. "There's going to be an all-camp bonfire, and no one would miss me."

"Oh," he said in a flat tone.

Jessica felt her spirits sinking. *He doesn't want to see me?* she wondered. She clutched the phone tightly against her ear and braced herself. "Paul, what's going on?"

"Well . . ." He hesitated. "I can't see you tomorrow, Jessica. My parents found out about the horse, and they're pretty mad."

She pushed her hair off her shoulder and switched the phone to her other ear. "When can you see me again?"

"I don't know," he said. "It's going to take them a few days to calm down over this."

"A few days! But Paul—"

"Listen, Jessica, I have to go right now. But I promise I'll come and see you as soon as humanly possible."

Jessica sighed as she hung up the phone. *Seems the only hot date lined up for my Friday night is with a bonfire*, she thought with a wry smile. *Goody, goody—silly songs, ghost stories, and s'mores.* But at least she had all the camp stuff to pass the time until she could see Paul again.

✿　　✿　　✿

46

The following evening Lila stood before the full-length mirror in the girls' bathroom, admiring her reflection. It had taken her hours, but she was finally ready for her date with Bo. She had skipped her last arts and crafts class of the day, claiming a terrible headache.

Stunning, she thought as she turned from side to side. She'd swept her hair up into an elegant twist, showcasing her diamond-and-ruby drop earrings. She'd decided to keep the jewelry simple; the earrings, a diamond pendant, and her gold-and-ruby ring provided just the right amount of sparkle to complement her dazzling beaded black gown. A pair of Italian black leather sandals and a beaded black bag added the finishing touches.

"Je suis belle," she chanted, telling herself she was beautiful. "Bo darling, look out," she added with a wink.

The door opened suddenly. Lila whirled around and saw Jessica watching her with an amused expression. "Talking to yourself again, I see," Jessica said. "And aren't we a bit overdressed for a camp bonfire?"

Lila shrugged innocently. "Oh, you mean this old thing?" They both laughed. Jessica was aware that the gown had cost a small fortune and that it was Lila's favorite. "I'm glad I didn't listen to you when you tried to talk me out of bringing it to camp," Lila said.

Jessica's gaze swept over her. "No offense, Lila, but you're going to look ridiculous showing up like that tonight."

"Not where I'm going." Lila turned back to the mirror and applied another coat of midnight-raspberry lipstick.

"Even if you're going out for dinner, there isn't a restaurant within a hundred miles that's fancy enough for that outfit."

Lila slipped the lipstick tube into her black beaded handbag. "Bo and I are doing Paris tonight."

"What?" Jessica's eyes flashed. "You can't just up and leave for France. That's not fair."

Lila laughed, enjoying the moment. "Bo is planning a surprise for me. I told him that I'd dreamed of us in Paris, and he said he'd create Paris in springtime for me right here, tonight."

Jessica sighed wistfully. "I'm not going to be able to see Paul until who knows when."

"I'm sure he'll come around as soon as he can," Lila said.

Jessica nodded. "I know. I just hope it's soon."

"Well, I've got to run. Don't eat too many s'mores tonight, Jess." Lila gathered her things and left, a huge, self-satisfied grin on her face. *There's nothing quite like a best friend's envy to sweeten an already delicious evening,* she reflected.

As Nicole walked to the main field for the all-camp bonfire, Derek Smith, a senior counselor, fell into step beside her. "You were looking pretty fantastic out on the lake this afternoon," he said. "Where did you learn to water-ski so well? I don't think I've ever seen anyone do a one-handed flip quite like that before."

"Thanks," she said, basking in the praise. "It was nothing. I do tricks like that all the time." She wasn't about to admit that her hand had slipped off the tow bar by mistake and that she'd nearly wiped out big-time.

"Hey, Nicole, wait up," Maria's voice called to her from behind. Nicole turned, then groaned to herself when she saw that Maria was with Elizabeth, who was wearing Joey's Yale sweatshirt again.

"I'll see you later," Derek said good-naturedly as he continued toward the field.

Nicole was tempted to ignore Maria and follow him. *He's not bad-looking,* she thought as she watched him walk away. Derek was the tumbling instructor, which was why he was in such great shape. He was tall, with collar-length blond hair and smoky blue eyes. And he definitely seemed interested in her. *Too bad he doesn't have light brown hair and green eyes,* she mused. *Too bad he isn't Joey.*

She waited for Maria and Elizabeth to catch up, forcing her expression to remain neutral. She had big plans, which wouldn't work if the wonder twin became the least bit suspicious.

"Let's all sit together," Maria said as they approached the crowd already gathered around a huge bonfire.

Dizzy Lizzie stuck her bottom lip between her teeth. "I think Jessica is expecting me to sit with her."

"She's over there with her group," Maria said, waving to Wakefield twin number two, who was surrounded by her devoted seven- and eight-year-old disciples. Maria pointed to an empty spot on the other side of the fire. "Let's sit over there. And I don't want to hear any arguments from either of you two. Just for once, you guys can be civil."

Nicole glanced at Elizabeth and shrugged. Elizabeth looked her in the eye, sending her a silent challenge. Nicole smiled and stared back at her. They held their gazes steady for several seconds, oblivious to everything around them.

Elizabeth was the first one to look away. Nicole mentally congratulated herself. *Watch out, wonder twin,* she thought. *You're way out of your league.*

They followed Maria and sat on either side of her.

The circle began to fill in as more and more

people arrived. Nicole looked around for Joey. When he finally arrived, he looked in her direction and waved, his whole face lighting up with a warm smile. Her heart skipped a beat—until she realized he was looking at Elizabeth.

Nicole was relieved when he took a seat with some of the other senior counselors on the other side of the circle. It would have been torture to sit through an entire evening watching Dizzy Lizzie hanging all over him.

Maria draped her arms across Nicole's and Elizabeth's shoulders. "Smile, girls!"

Nicole looked up and saw eight-year-old Maggie pointing her video camera at them. Seething inside, she forced herself to make laughing noises. Nicole still hated the little stinker for exposing her theft of Elizabeth's play.

What was the big deal, anyway? Nicole asked herself. Writers were always rehashing old story plots. *West Side Story* was a remake of *Romeo and Juliet,* for Pete's sake. For that matter, Elizabeth's own play was only a retelling of the old camp legend.

Lacey officially began the bonfire ceremony the same way she did everything else—by banging on her pot with a spoon. Some of the campers performed skits they'd worked on in Joey and Maria's drama workshops. Two girls sang a duet. Rose and

Suzanne taught the group some new songs, accompanying the sing-along with their guitars. Winston Egbert told some corny jokes. Marshmallows, chocolate, and graham crackers were passed around so the campers could make s'mores.

As the night got darker the campers began clamoring for a ghost story. Nicole spoke up. "Hey, Joey, why don't you tell them all about Crazy Freddy?"

Joey smiled at *her*—not at Elizabeth, she was certain—and readily agreed. He moved closer to the fire, where everyone could see him, and began. "I love telling this story, but are you guys sure you want to know about Crazy Freddy?" He frowned and shook his head. "Might be hard for some of the little ones to handle. Maybe we should wait until—"

A collective groan rose from the group, urging him to continue. He raised his hands and gestured for silence. Nicole loved watching him. She'd heard the story many times, but she never got tired of listening to Joey. He was a natural storyteller, using his hands, his face, and his voice to make the tale come to life.

After I get rid of the wonder twin, Joey will realize that I'm the one who truly loves him, Nicole thought. She smiled softly, watching the way the firelight played across his features as he spoke.

He will be mine again, very soon, she promised herself.

Joey looked around the circle. "Do you remember what Lacey told us a few weeks ago about that woodsman who used to work here, the one who fell in love with the head counselor? Like Lacey said, they both disappeared one night and were never seen again. But that's not really where the story ends." He paused, creating dramatic tension.

"You see, a few years ago someone saw evidence of a fire in the woodsman's abandoned cabin. The police checked it out, but no one was found. Then another time, some hunters found something else. . . ."

He shuddered. After another long pause, he continued. "At first they thought it might be the remains of a deer or an antelope that poachers had left behind—but then they spotted a pair of high-top sneakers poking out from under a bush. Deer and antelope don't wear shoes, do they?"

A few murmurs of "no" rose from the campers.

Joey's voice dropped to a stage whisper. "One of the hunters bent down to pick up the shoes. They seemed awfully heavy." He opened his eyes wide and raised his voice. "The feet were still in them, cut off at the ankles!"

Several people in the group gasped, and not just the little kids. Nicole chuckled softly.

"Then," Joey continued, "the police came and found more body parts—*human* body parts. Everyone tried to believe it was an isolated incident—until a group of hikers, four or five of them, got lost on Echo Mountain one night. They heard the sound of somebody chopping wood. Hoping to find someone who could point them in the right direction to get back to their camp, they followed the sound."

Joey closed his eyes and shook his head. "Only one of them returned—covered with blood, shaking hysterically. His hands had been chopped off, and he kept saying over and over, 'Crazy Freddy, Crazy Freddy, Crazy Freddy. . . .' To this day, they are the only words he speaks."

Joey's voice took on a warning tone. "Every once in a while, you can still hear the sound of someone chopping wood deep in the forest late at night. Be very careful. It's no ghost, believe me. It's Crazy Freddy."

The crowd was silent, the flames casting eerie shadows on everyone's face. Nicole smiled as she saw Elizabeth shudder. *I think the time has come for the wonder twin to meet Crazy Freddy—one on one.*

Nestled in Bo's arms, Lila sighed contentedly. "Let's see, what's my favorite spot in the whole world? That's a tough one."

They were lying together on a blanket underneath the stars, relaxing after the best French meal Lila had ever eaten in her life. The air was sweetly scented by the hundreds of fresh flowers that Bo had ordered for the occasion. Nearby, the musicians he'd hired played a romantic duet for violin and cello. Lila found herself forgetting they were Buford and Johansen, two gangly junior counselors from Pittsburgh. Their incredible talent made up for their lack of social grace and style.

"I don't know if I could name any one particular place," Lila said, after some thought. "It would depend on what sort of mood I was in. If I felt like skiing, it could be Aspen, or if I felt like working on my tan, it might be a warm Caribbean island— or an ocean cruise."

"I prefer skiing in Switzerland," Bo said, absently stroking Lila's elbow. "But as much as I love Europe, I have to admit that all the best beaches on the continent are overcrowded."

Lila marveled at how much Bo knew about the world, and that he cared enough to want to bring it to her. She was touched by all he'd done to give her Paris in springtime. The flower delivery alone had required two separate trips by Western Meadowlark.

"What about you, Bo?" she asked. "Do you have a favorite spot in the whole world?"

He flashed that gorgeous, sexy smile of his. "Wherever you are, Lila. That's the only place I'd want to be."

She giggled, glowing with pleasure. "OK, let's say you could take me with you. Where would we go?"

"I've already been everywhere I've ever wanted to go. No, wait—I know exactly where I'd take you."

Lila raised her eyebrows. "Where?"

"It's a magical place," he said, rolling over onto his back. "Last year I played a sailor in my school's production of *South Pacific*. It was kind of fun. That's the reason I picked Camp Echo Mountain from the list of camps my father gave me." Bo had originally told Lila that his father had forced him to attend camp in the hope that it would "make a man out of him."

Lila thought Bo was all the man she'd ever need.

"Anyway," he continued, "*South Pacific* is mostly singing and dancing—not much of an intellectual challenge. But in the story, there's this island called Bali Ha'i, where the sailors are forbidden to go."

"And that's where you want to go?" Lila asked.

Bo grinned sheepishly. "Yeah. Silly, huh? I don't even know if it really exists."

Lila propped herself up on her elbow and looked into his gorgeous brown eyes. "I don't think it's silly at all. It's . . . creative."

He chuckled. "I'll show you creative," he whispered, and he gently pulled her down for a deep, passionate kiss.

The following morning Jessica groaned as Lila babbled on and on about her date with Bo, gloating over every little detail. They were brushing their teeth in the girls' bathroom, sharing a sink because the room was crowded.

"And the dessert—you wouldn't believe it!" Lila gushed, spewing white foam from her mouth. "We had this delicious sundae called a Mont Blanc, made from the richest vanilla ice cream and chestnut sauce, topped with freshly whipped cream."

Jessica mumbled something vague, scrubbing her teeth vigorously with frustrated energy.

"There were fresh flowers everywhere. Bo must have bought out every florist in the county. It was so perfect." Lila stopped talking as she swished around a mouthful of mouthwash, giving Jessica a few moments of relief.

Jessica studied her reflection in the mirror and tried to decide whether to wear her hair down or up. Down was sexy, but up would keep her neck cool. *I wonder if Paul is going to show up today,* she thought.

Lila spit and capped the mouthwash bottle. "We're doing Moroccan tonight. Bo ordered couscous and chicken from this wonderful place we both love in New York. I'm so glad you talked me into coming here, Jess. Camp Echo Mountain is turning out to be more fun than the Riviera, Aspen, and the Caribbean all rolled together."

"That's nice, Lila," Jessica grumbled.

Chapter 5

Elizabeth took a long, hot shower before bed Saturday night, hoping it would help her to relax. A hazy premonition of danger seemed to be following her day and night. *But it doesn't make sense*, she thought, whipping up a frothy lather of rose-scented shampoo. She considered how peaceful the camp had become in the last few days. Except for the excitement about the upcoming color war, everyone seemed exceptionally calm. Her sailing workshops were going much more smoothly now. Rose Schwartz, the instructor, seemed willing to forget Elizabeth's disastrous beginning.

Elizabeth closed her eyes, letting the warm water cascade over her body. Everything was going fine. Even Jessica and Nicole were behaving themselves.

This is only the calm before the storm, a small, frightened voice inside her warned.

Jessica floated on her back, gazing at the stars in the black sky. A bright quarter moon, as yellow as a lemon slice, seemed to be suspended only a few feet above the lake. The water was perfect—cool and soothing after a long, hot day. *I'm thoroughly happy,* she thought.

Lila surfaced next to her, breaking the spell. "I don't know how much more of this place I can stand. I think I'm having civilization withdrawal. I swear I'd give anything to see the inside of a mall."

Jessica chuckled, only half listening. "Paul has never seen the ocean," she said. "Maybe some-day—" She swallowed the rest of the sentence. She didn't want to make plans for the future, as she had done with Christian. His death had taught her that life was for living one moment at a time.

Lila slammed her palm on the surface of the water, splashing Jessica's face. "Wake up, Jess. This camp is driving me insane. And I'm turning into a prune." She turned and headed for shore.

Jessica decided she'd also had enough and followed. As they emerged from the water Lila slapped her thigh with a loud smack. "These mosquitoes! I'm telling you, between the bugs and the—what *is* that annoying sound?"

"That's a loon." Jessica grabbed her towel from where she'd left it hanging on a low branch and wrapped it turban-style around her head. "Paul says they used to be very rare, but they've been making a comeback in this area over the last few years."

Lila arched her eyebrows. "Aren't *you* the nature girl all of a sudden."

"Come on, Lila. You're just mad because Bo stood you up tonight."

Lila flashed her a look of indignation. "He did not! It wasn't his fault that he got in trouble for hiring out his daily chores. Lacey's so uptight about rules. Can you believe he's stuck with kitchen duty for the rest of the month?" She yanked her fluffy green monogrammed towel off its branch and wrapped it around her shoulders. "I mean, it's not like his work went undone. And he was *providing jobs*. This is so unfair. Now we'll never be able to have dinner together again."

Jessica hid her smile. "Sounds tough."

Lila slapped her leg again. "I'm getting out of here. These creatures are eating me alive."

"I think I'll stay out here for a while longer," Jessica said.

"Suit yourself," Lila said with a sniff as she walked away.

Jessica took a deep breath of the fresh mountain

air. *If only Paul were here,* she thought. She wondered what he was doing at that very moment. Was he still at the restaurant, maybe cleaning the grill or mopping the kitchen floor?

Suddenly an arm wrapped around her and a large hand covered her mouth. Her heart stopped for a split second, then began thumping with a fierce, pounding beat. She tried to scream, but her voice came out muffled. She was being dragged backward. Struggling with all her might, she jerked and kicked and dug her fingernails into whatever flesh she could reach. She was pulled into the boathouse, fighting desperately the whole way.

Once she was inside, the arms around her loosened. She whirled around, prepared for battle—but not for the shock of recognition. *Paul?* Before she could react, his lips took hers in a heart-stopping kiss.

For a moment Jessica let herself sink into the kiss. Then she shoved him away, hard. "Are you crazy, scaring me like that?" she screamed.

Paul ducked his head sheepishly. "I'm sorry, Jessica. When you started kicking and scratching, I was afraid you'd alert the whole camp. I just wanted to surprise you."

"You sure did that." Jessica giggled. "I'm going to have to stop listening to those ghost stories, or else I'll turn into a nervous wreck. Last night we heard one about an ax murderer named Crazy Freddy who goes around chopping up hikers."

"I promise I won't ever sneak up on you again." Paul rubbed the scratches on his arms and gave her a lopsided grin. "For my own sake," he added.

"OK, you're forgiven." She stepped back into his arms and sighed contentedly. He even smelled sexy, an enticing scent that was a combination of warm male and clean shirt, with a touch of pine forest. "I can't believe you're really here," she said. "How did you manage to get by Lacey?"

Paul brushed his lips against her forehead. "I came in from the other side of the lake. There's a service road that ends a mile or so from camp. I left my truck there and hiked the rest of the way."

Jessica tipped her head back and flashed him a coy smile. "All that, just to see me?"

"Just call me Crazy Paul," he said, lowering his lips to hers again.

Elizabeth squinted against the bright midday sun and clapped her hands for attention. She had the seven- and eight-year-old girls, Jessica's Wanna-bes, out on the lake for a sailing lesson. Rose was standing against the stern, letting Elizabeth take full charge of the class for the first time.

"Now girls, who can tell me what a jib sheet is?" Elizabeth asked. She tried to ignore the fact that

Maggie was videotaping her. "Sofia, do you know the answer?" She turned to the girl with huge brown eyes and dark corkscrew curls.

Before Sofia could answer, her older sister, Anastasia, spoke up. She was a slightly taller version of Sofia, but with blue eyes. "The red team is going to make dog food out of the blue team," she said.

Tanya, who was Paul's little sister and Jessica's most devoted follower, pulled one of Anastasia's corkscrew curls and said, "Shut up, stupid. Everybody on the red team is going to end up in a body bag."

Elizabeth took a deep breath and counted to ten. "Girls, the color war is just for fun."

Sarah, a Chinese American girl with shoulder-length black hair, waved her hand in the air as if she were flagging down a classroom teacher. "Yeah, but the blue team is going to win because we're the best, right, Elizabeth?"

Before Elizabeth could respond, Stephanie, an energetic girl with frizzy red hair, began to jump up and down, her green eyes flashing. "Yeth, yeth, yeth, the blue team ith going to win, win, win!" She had trouble pronouncing some words because her two front teeth were missing.

"It doesn't matter who wins," Elizabeth said firmly. "Good sportsmanship is the most important thing. I think all of you know that."

The girls nodded solemnly, but Elizabeth doubted her words would have any lasting effect.

She could hardly blame them. Everyone in the camp was excited about the color war. After the flag raising ceremony that morning, Nicole had announced that to show its solidarity, the red team would be wearing its color for the rest of the week. Elizabeth would have preferred to downplay the competition, but she'd gone ahead and declared that the blue team would also wear its color.

A bright flash of light on the shore caught her attention. She looked and saw Nicole standing there, watching her through a pair of binoculars, the sunlight reflecting off the lenses. Feeling like a bug under a microscope, Elizabeth shuddered. *The color war is just for fun,* she repeated to herself.

"Are you sure you don't want to join Elizabeth and me for a swim?" Maria asked Nicole as they walked out of the mess hall after dinner that evening.

Nicole adjusted her red baseball cap and glanced across the lake. Spending extra time with Elizabeth Wakefield was the last thing she wanted to do. Besides, she had to take care of something much more important. "Thanks, Maria, but I don't feel up to it. I'm really tired." She yawned for effect. "I think I'll just sit out here on the porch for a while and watch the sun go down."

"We could do something else." Maria turned to her with a measuring look. "Or is it because of Elizabeth that you don't want to go swimming?"

Nicole stopped and put her hands on her hips. "I would go swimming if I wanted to, whether Elizabeth did or not."

"That's good," Maria said. "I hate having to choose between you two."

"No problem." Nicole sat in one of the rocking chairs on the porch and looked up at Maria. "Actually, Elizabeth and I have reached a sort of understanding," she said. *It's partly true,* Nicole reasoned. *I understand that Elizabeth is selfish, grabby, and worthless, and soon she'll understand that I'm not someone to mess with.*

"Thanks," Maria said. "I know it hasn't been easy for you." Nicole yawned again as she began to rock slowly. "Don't worry about me. I'll be fine. You go have a nice swim." She sighed with relief when Maria finally left.

A few minutes later, Nicole headed down the path that led to the boys' cabins, which were located on the opposite side of the lake from the girls'. She knew that Joey was in the drama cabin, checking the props, and that the other senior counselors were also preparing for the following day's workshops.

When Nicole arrived at the male senior counselors' cabin, she suffered a moment of doubt, but she pushed herself forward, reminding herself it was for a worthy cause. The cabin was decorated much the same as the girls', but instead of faded flowery curtains, the guys had faded stripes. The smell was also different, a mixture of old sneakers and spicy aftershave lotion.

Five senior counselors shared the cabin. Nicole wandered around the room, looking at the stuff scattered on the dressers and nightstands, trying to decide which unit belonged to Joey. There was a stack of books on the floor next to one of the beds. Craning her neck, she skimmed the titles. *The Actor's Craft, Shakespearean Theater, The Collected Works of Henrik Ibsen.* "I think I've found you, Joey," she whispered.

Feeling a sense of growing excitement, Nicole searched through his things. Finally, in the bottom drawer of his dresser, she found what she'd been looking for—and without a moment's hesitation, she took it.

In the counselors' recreation room, the tapping suddenly stopped and a dozen bodies sprang out of their chairs, groping for the spoons on the table. Aaron yelled, "Winston's out!"

Elizabeth yawned in spite of the frenzy. She'd hoped that Joey would show up, but after playing spoons for nearly an hour, she was ready to give up for the night. The stress of breaking up arguments over the color war all day long had taken its toll— not to mention worrying about Jessica, feeling guilty about Todd, and looking over her shoulder for Nicole.

"Here, Winston, you can have mine." Elizabeth tossed him her white plastic spoon.

"Thanks. That's the nicest thing anyone has ever done for me," Winston joked.

"You want me to go with you, Liz?" Maria offered.

Elizabeth shook her head. "I'm fine. I just need to go to sleep."

Outside, Elizabeth nearly tripped over two people who were huddled together in the shadows next to the porch. Justin Siena, another JC from California, and Angela Davis, one of Elizabeth's cabinmates from New York, broke apart suddenly. Angela giggled, her large brown eyes wide with a look of surprise. "Hi, Elizabeth. Nice night for a walk."

"Sorry, I didn't see you guys there," Elizabeth murmured.

"That was the idea," Justin said.

Elizabeth apologized again and continued on her way to her cabin. Seeing Justin and Angela together had made her feel worse. *I miss Joey so much,* she thought.

By the time she'd finished brushing her teeth in

the girls' bathroom, Elizabeth felt utterly worn out and sleepy. She returned to her cabin and pulled Joey's sweatshirt out of her drawer. *Maybe I'll even get a decent night's sleep,* she thought, glancing at her bed, which looked inviting.

She noticed a yellow envelope sticking out from under her pillow. Bemused, she pulled it out and tore it open. There was a note inside written on Joey's personalized stationery. Elizabeth smiled as she read the invitation to meet him behind the boathouse after lights-out.

Elizabeth's heart fluttered excitedly as she slipped the note back into the envelope and tucked it under her pillow. Suddenly she didn't feel tired at all.

She got into bed fully dressed and pulled the covers up to her chin. Hugging Joey's sweatshirt to her chest, she closed her eyes. And waited.

Hours later, deep in the night, a pair of bright eyes watched as a girl made her way through the dark forest. A long blond braid hung down her slender back. She appeared to be in a hurry, her steps quick and eager.

The eyes followed her, keeping her locked in their gaze. They were the eyes of a predator, glistening with delight at having spotted easy prey.

Smiling, the watcher advanced.

Chapter 6

The sound of the wind whistling through the trees grew louder and more sinister as Elizabeth crept deeper into the woods. She had the uneasy feeling that someone was watching her. Steeling herself, she wrapped Joey's sweatshirt more tightly around her and kept on going.

A twig snapped nearby. Elizabeth stopped in her tracks, her heart pounding. Holding her breath, she turned on her flashlight and scanned the darkness for any signs of danger. *There's nothing out there but tall trees and small, harmless forest creatures,* she assured herself.

Then she heard something else—the clop of an ax chopping wood. Her imagination began to whirl in a kaleidoscope of gruesome visions. *Missing hikers . . . dead bodies in the woods . . . Crazy Freddy . . .*

Get a grip! she ordered herself. She reminded herself that Crazy Freddy was only a silly campfire story. Suddenly, out of the corner of her eye, she caught a glimpse of something moving. She turned quickly and saw a shadowy figure dressed in a flowing dark robe swinging an ax behind a grove of trees.

Elizabeth opened her mouth and screamed. Afraid for her life, she turned and ran.

Doubled over with laughter, Nicole pulled the blanket off her head and dropped the rusty ax on the ground. *What a stupid twit!* she thought. She couldn't believe Elizabeth had fallen for such a dumb trick.

But Nicole didn't allow herself to stand around and celebrate her victory. Even someone as brain-dead as Dizzy Lizzie would eventually figure out who was behind this cute little trick—especially if she showed the forged note to Joey.

Nicole bundled up her blanket and headed back to the cabin. Once she got rid of the note, there wouldn't be any evidence pointing to her.

Halfway to her cabin, Elizabeth stopped running and ordered herself to be reasonable. After all, this was a camp. Chopping wood at camp wasn't so strange. It could have been a staff member working late, replenishing the camp's supply of firewood.

And she might even have seen something as innocent as a tree swaying in the breeze. The night was awfully dark. She'd also been under a lot of strain and hadn't been getting enough sleep. It was possible that her imagination had gone wild for those few minutes.

Summoning her courage, she turned around and marched back to the boathouse. But Joey wasn't there.

Frustrated, Elizabeth gazed across the lake and wondered if he'd given up on her. *Well, I'm not ready to give up!* she thought. Determined to see Joey, she made up her mind to go to his cabin.

She didn't feel brave enough to paddle a canoe across the lake to the boys' side by herself, which meant she'd have to walk all the way around the large kidney-shaped lake. *Joey is worth it,* she told herself.

She briskly made her way along the wooded path that followed the shore of the lake. When she reached the main area of camp, she slowed down, taking care not to step on any dry leaves or twigs that would give her away. *I can't believe I'm doing this,* Elizabeth thought. She'd lost count of how many rules she'd broken since coming to camp.

The spotlight outside the main lodge cast eerie shadows across the path. The rustic cabins where the indoor workshops were held during the day stood still and lifeless. Elizabeth felt as if she were creeping through a ghost town.

As she passed the small white house where Lacey lived, Elizabeth heard the scraping sound of a window opening. She ducked behind a tree and held her breath, hoping the shadows would keep her hidden from view.

Lacey stuck her head out the second-floor window. "What do you think you're doing?" she asked sharply. "Come out from behind that tree, young lady. I'm in no mood for childish games."

Elizabeth gulped and, trying not to look guilty, did as she was ordered.

Lacey glared down at her. "I'm waiting for an explanation, young lady."

"Well, I was just . . . um . . ." Elizabeth didn't know what to say. She couldn't tell the truth—that she'd been wandering around at eleven at night and heard chopping-wood noises, which caused her to miss her date with Joey, so she'd decided to visit him in his cabin instead.

Lacey continued to scowl at her, pinning Elizabeth with her eyes. Defeated, Elizabeth lowered her head. Without another word, she turned around and headed back to her cabin.

Elizabeth slipped off her shoes before she entered the cabin and padded to her bed in stocking feet. It occurred to her how strange it was to be sneaking in late, while Jessica, the adventurous twin, lay curled up under the covers, sleeping soundly.

Nicole was also in bed, her red baseball cap on the floor next to her nightstand. Lila was softly snoring, and across the cabin Angela murmured something in her sleep.

Elizabeth crawled under the covers without bothering to undress. *What happened to Joey tonight?* she wondered. Lying on her back with her eyes closed, she pictured him easily—his light brown hair falling over his forehead, his sexy lips, the way his green eyes would light up when he laughed.

Suddenly, like a bucket of ice water splashed on her head, the image of Todd's face appeared, his expression cold and distant. *What am I doing?* she thought as tears spilled down her face. She didn't understand how she could be cheating on Todd, whom she'd loved for ages.

Love? Ha! her conscience jeered. She hadn't written to Todd in weeks, still hadn't sent him a thank-you for the lovely care package. She hadn't even opened the box of stationery he'd sent.

Nothing made sense anymore. The only thing she knew was that she was desperate to see Joey again. Elizabeth buried her face in his sweatshirt.

Why didn't he wait for me tonight? she wondered.

She slipped her hand under the pillow to get his note, but she couldn't find it. Frowning, she flipped over the pillow. The note wasn't there.

Elizabeth jumped out of bed and searched through the sheets. *What did I do with it?* she wondered, straining to remember. She checked her pockets, then turned on her flashlight and searched through her nightstand, under the bed, in her bathroom bag. Joey's note had disappeared!

Nicole! Elizabeth thought. She looked across the room at Nicole, who lay curled up on her side, burrowed under the covers. With a groan of frustration Elizabeth got back into bed and pulled the blanket over her head. "There *was* a note, wasn't there?" she whispered. She wasn't sure anymore. Maybe she'd only dreamed that she'd found a note.

A cold shiver ran through her. The creepy sound of someone chopping wood in the forest haunted her mind. She tried to reassure herself that everything was all right, but her mind kept shouting, *No, it isn't!* In her gut, she knew there was something out there, something evil.

Elizabeth squeezed her eyes shut, sure she'd spend the rest of the night dreaming of Crazy Freddy.

The following morning Jessica stood at the door

of the Wanna-bes' cabin, her temper stretched to the breaking point. The place was a madhouse, with feathers flying and kids jumping on the beds.

The senior counselors took turns staying in the younger campers' cabins overnight and helping them get ready in the morning. Rose, who'd had wanna-be duty the previous night, had asked Jessica to take over for her in the morning because she had an early meeting with Lacey.

Jessica had arrived a few minutes late, which seemed to have given the Wanna-bes just enough time to trash their cabin. "What's going on here?" Jessica shouted.

All action stopped. Six pairs of wide, frightened eyes turned to her. "She started it," Anastasia said, pointing an accusing finger at Sarah. "She said the red team sucks raw eggs."

"I did not," Sarah said, shaking her straight dark hair out of her eyes. "It was your dumb sister who started it. Sofia threw her shoes at me."

Jessica stepped inside and slammed the door shut. As the day of the color war drew nearer, the excitement of everyone at camp was growing stronger. *More than these rug rats can handle, apparently,* she thought hotly. "I don't care who started it," she said, giving each of them a stern look. "You're all to blame. Just look at this mess!"

The girls hung their heads in disgrace.

"No one is leaving this cabin until it's completely clean and every last feather is picked up," Jessica said. "Do you hear me?"

They all nodded.

She reached for the doorknob. "I'm going to send word that this cabin isn't going to make it to the flag raising ceremony this morning, and then I'm coming right back. And when I do, this place had better be on its way to being set right."

"We're really sorry," Maggie murmured.

Sofia sniffed. "Do you still like us, Jessica?"

Jessica exhaled loudly. "I'm not sure right now."

"I like your hair like that, Jessica," Tanya said timidly.

"I like your hair, too," Anastasia said. Stephanie, Sofia, Sarah, and Maggie chimed in as well.

Jessica rolled her eyes. "Thanks." *What a bunch of kiss-ups!* she thought, raising her fingers to her lips to hide her smile. "Now get to work."

When she returned, she found the girls had made an effort to put the cabin back together. Most of their clothes had been picked up off the floor. Sarah, Tanya, and Anastasia had made their beds. Jessica had borrowed a vacuum cleaner from the main lodge, and she let the girls take turns chasing after the wispy flecks of down.

When everything was back in shape, Jessica nodded with approval. "This is more like it. Now I suggest you hurry up and get dressed, or you'll miss breakfast, too."

Tanya handed her a blue ribbon and a covered elastic band. "Can you make my hair like yours?" she asked.

"I guess," Jessica said. Because the weather was supposed to be hot and sunny that day, she'd decided to wear her hair in a chignon at the back of her head. She should have guessed that it would cause a stir of excitement among the Wanna-bes.

"But what about my friendship bracelet, the one you made for me?" Tanya asked. "Can I still wear it, even if it's purple? It might not go with the blue ribbon."

"I'm sure it will be all right," Jessica said. She ordered Tanya to turn around and began twisting her dyed brown hair into a tight coil.

"The buckle is coming undone," Tanya said, waving her wrist in Jessica's face.

"Watch it," Jessica said, grasping Tanya's hand. She looked closely and saw that she'd missed a few loops when she'd woven the clasp into the brace- let. "I'll fix it later," she told Tanya.

"I'm going to make you one just like it, Jessica, so we can be twins," Tanya said.

"Elizabeth is her twin," Sarah said.

"I am, too," Tanya said. She was the most devoted

of the Wanna-bes and had once gone so far as to bleach her hair to match Jessica's.

Jessica giggled to herself as she recalled the day she and Paul had first met, when he had come to camp to take Tanya to a family outing. He'd gone ballistic over his sister's bleached hair, aiming most of his fury at Jessica. She could still picture the way his dark eyes had flashed at her like lightning bolts.

Since then, Paul Mathis had become a permanent thought in Jessica's mind. *I just hope I get to see him again soon,* she thought.

When Jessica was finished arranging Tanya's hair, Maggie held out her hairbrush and a red ribbon. "I'm next," Maggie said. "But I have to have a red ribbon because of the color war. I don't think it's fair that I can't be on your team."

"Those are the rules," Jessica said, hurrying to get Maggie's hair done. But when Jessica looked up, she saw that the other girls were standing in line, holding their hairbrushes and ribbons. "Don't tell me I have to do everyone's hair this morning!"

"Only do the blue team," Sarah said.

Sofia stuck her tongue out at her. "Go suck an egg, Sarah."

Stephanie, always full of energy, shoved Sofia, who in turn screamed and shoved back, knocking Tanya against a dresser. Jessica filled her lungs and yelled in her deepest, loudest cheerleader voice, "*Stop it right now!*" Six little girls froze like statues.

"That's better," Jessica said. "If I hear one more sound out of you girls, no one is going to wear their hair like mine. Understood?" Barely breathing, they nodded. Jessica smiled, impressed with herself.

When the girls finally made it to breakfast, the mess hall was a sea of red and blue, with everyone dressed in team colors.

Jessica spotted her sister in the food line. Like her, Elizabeth was wearing a pair of khaki shorts and a blue T-shirt, with her hair pulled into a chignon. Jessica realized that she and Elizabeth were one hundred percent identical that day. *This could come in handy,* she mused.

As she picked up a clean tray and took her place in the food line, Jessica's mind was already working up a wonderful idea for Saturday.

That evening Elizabeth mumbled to herself as she walked to the lodge for dinner. A group of campers ran past her, laughing and yelling, but she barely noticed. Her mind was in a jumble, trying to sort out what was happening. *Did Joey leave that note under my pillow . . . or was it another one of Nicole's dirty tricks?* she asked herself over and over.

When she had questioned Joey about the note that afternoon, he'd looked at her as if she were crazy. He'd had no idea what she was talking about and couldn't even remember the last time he'd used his personalized stationery.

So if it wasn't Joey who left the note . . . Elizabeth rolled the possibilities over in her mind. *It had to be Nicole.*

But Nicole hadn't been acting the least bit suspiciously. Elizabeth decided that she must have dreamed most of what had happened the night before—the note, the shadowy figure in the woods, maybe even the chopping noise. *All this fresh air must be going to my head,* she thought. And yet it had all seemed so real. There had to be a logical explanation.

Logical? the rational part of her brain questioned. *Yeah, right.* Seeing a ghostly figure wielding an ax in the woods wasn't very logical at all.

When she reached the main lodge, she plopped down in a rocking chair on the front porch. *I guess it was all Crazy Freddy's doing,* she thought wryly. Maybe she would be the one to disappear with him this time around. *Who knows? If I'm lucky, I can become part of the old legend, and the name of Elizabeth Wakefield will live on forever in campfire lore.*

"Well, that proves it," she sighed as she rocked back and forth. "I'm losing my grip on reality."

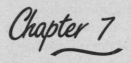

Chapter 7

"I can't remember ever *not* wanting to be a writer," Elizabeth said pensively as she dangled her feet off the dock into the cool water. "I think I was scribbling stories with crayons on scraps of paper even before I could speak."

Floating on his back a few feet from the dock, Joey chuckled. "I hope you'll write more plays. You have a real knack for creating emotional tension and natural-sounding dialogue."

Elizabeth's face flushed with pleasure. "Thanks."

She was glad that Joey had persuaded her to meet him after lights-out for a late-night swim. The evening was so beautiful and peaceful. A gibbous moon hung over the shimmering lake; somewhere in the distance, a coyote howled mournfully.

"I'd like to write another one someday," Elizabeth

said. "I suppose I will when another great idea comes along and inspires me, like Lacey's woodsman legend."

Joey feigned a hurt expression. "You mean my Crazy Freddy story didn't?"

Elizabeth laughed and kicked her foot, splashing him. "It scared me." Remembering how afraid she'd been in the woods the night before, her smile faded.

Joey picked up on her changed mood instantly. "What's wrong?" he asked gently.

Elizabeth exhaled a shaky sigh. "I don't want to talk about it, Joey. I must have had a crazy dream last night. Maybe I was sleepwalking." She forced herself to smile, and then told him about the chopping noises she heard the night before. "I hope you have nothing against dating girls who are going crazy."

He playfully splashed her legs. "Not if you let me go crazy with you." His expression became serious. "I care about you so much, Elizabeth. I'm really sorry I wasn't out here to meet you last night. I feel like I let you down."

"No, Joey, don't think that. Being with you is so—" She paused, searching for the right words to tell him how he made her feel. But how could she describe the bittersweet joy and passion, the way her heart would leap whenever she'd see him or hear his name? Or the yearning she felt when he wasn't around?

Suddenly Elizabeth's whole body tensed. The

sound of someone chopping wood was coming from somewhere nearby. *And I'm wide awake this time!* she thought.

Joey frowned. "What is it, Elizabeth?"

"Can't you hear it?" she cried.

He lifted his head out of the water and gripped the edge of the dock, holding himself still. "Yeah, I hear it," he said, pulling himself up onto the dock. "I have a feeling your Crazy Freddy is our pal Nicole. She probably didn't see me in the water and thought you were out here by yourself." He grabbed his flashlight and cursed. "I think it's time for this little game of hers to end." Not bothering with his towel or shoes, he took off, running barefoot and dripping wet into the woods.

Elizabeth wrapped her arms around her legs and tucked her knees under her chin. Joey's red T-shirt lay in a heap on the dock, where he'd tossed it earlier. Elizabeth touched the soft fabric, smiling. *Thank goodness he was here,* she thought, relishing the warm feeling of having someone to watch over her. *And thank goodness I'm not going nuts!*

A few minutes later Joey returned. "I didn't catch her," he said as he sat down beside Elizabeth. "But I saw someone in a red T-shirt running away."

"Nicole?" Elizabeth asked.

"It sure looked like her," he said, reaching for his towel.

Elizabeth felt a surge of hot anger. "How could anyone do something so mean?"

Joey kissed Elizabeth's forehead and slipped his red T-shirt over his head. "I don't think this is her only trick," he said as he finished putting on his T-shirt. "I'd also bet she was the one who left that forged note under your pillow. She must've stolen my stationery."

Elizabeth gazed into the woods, thinking of how terrified she had been the night before. Her blood felt as if it were boiling. *How dare Nicole treat me this way!*

Alone in her cabin the following afternoon, Nicole sat hunched over the scarred wooden desk, finishing her letter to Todd Wilkins.

"'. . . I know you trusted Elizabeth, and I'm sorry to have to give you the bad news,'" she read aloud. "'But you're such a cool guy, and I thought you ought to know.'" *This should do it,* she thought, smiling. She debated whether to sign off with "Love, Nicole."

She giggled. Maybe that would be going a bit too far. She settled for "Fondly" and signed her name with a flourish. *I'd say this letter proves I'm a great writer!* Nicole thought.

She picked up the photo she was also sending to Todd, a snapshot of Elizabeth and Joey kissing by the lake. The picture was clear, and she'd captured them perfectly. *And I'm a dynamite photographer, too!* she added.

Chuckling softly, she slipped the picture into the envelope and sealed it shut. Without a qualm, she walked over to Elizabeth's nightstand and rummaged around until she found several letters with Todd's return address. Unable to resist, Nicole sat on Elizabeth's bed and read each one.

They were filled with chatty things about what he was doing, people he'd met at basketball camp. Most of it was boring but cute. "You're too good for her, Todd," Nicole whispered. She had met him just about two weeks before, when he had visited the camp. He had actually driven all the way from southern California to Montana just to see Elizabeth, never knowing that his little princess was fooling around behind his back.

Nicole had warned Elizabeth weeks before that unless Elizabeth stopped seeing Joey, she would tell Todd all about him. At first Elizabeth had done right by her and had broken up with Joey. For six glorious days he and Nicole had been a couple, meeting for late-night dates at the boathouse, splashing about in the lake, and walking to meals hand in hand. It had been heavenly. But of course Elizabeth, being the dirty, rotten, lying cheat that she was, had gone back on her word and ruined everything.

Nicole's face grew hot with anger. *You may be Miss Popularity now, Dizzy Lizzie, but just you wait!* By the end of camp, the wonder twin would go from two guys to no guys.

Elizabeth sat at a picnic table near the main lodge, trying to write a letter to Todd. Before she'd left Sweet Valley, she'd promised to write to him at least every other day. But it had turned out to be just another one of her empty promises, along with "You can trust me" and "I love you."

She had never meant to be cruel. She owed him a letter, at the very least. *OK, so write it!* she ordered herself.

Instead she absently chewed on the cap of her ballpoint pen, gazed across the lake, ran her finger over the embossed silver *E* on the soft blue stationery he'd sent her. And found herself with absolutely nothing to say.

"Writers' block," she grumbled. *More like guilty-conscience block,* a voice inside her said.

She squeezed her eyes shut. Here she was, writing a letter to Todd while she cheated on him with Joey—it was something Jessica would do. Yet Elizabeth knew she wouldn't stop seeing Joey. Nor was she willing to give up Todd.

She gripped the pen more tightly and forced herself to concentrate on the task. She began by thanking Todd for the package he'd sent and for thinking of her. Then she moved on to describe what was generally going on at Camp Echo Mountain, making sure to emphasize how busy she was with sailing workshops and watching over her group of campers.

As she wrote the words "I miss you, Todd," Elizabeth realized they were true. She did love him and wanted him to be there for her when she returned to Sweet Valley. Losing him would hurt her deeply.

A tear rolled down her cheek and fell, creating a damp smudge on the letter. Her heart felt as if it were being torn apart. Elizabeth closed her eyes and sighed. When she opened them again, she saw Joey walking toward her, waving.

Elizabeth waved back, then hastily signed her letter and stuffed it into the matching blue envelope. She scribbled Todd's address, then tucked the envelope under her arm as she jumped up to go meet Joey.

I feel like I'm stuck on a never-ending roller coaster, she thought. *I just hope everything works out back at Sweet Valley High after this crazy summer ends.*

Nicole walked into the camp office later that afternoon with a big grin on her face. She wished she could be there when Todd read her letter. As she opened the wicker basket that served as the camp mailbox, a pale blue envelope with a silver *E* caught her eye. Nicole glanced at the address and chuckled. "The princess finally wrote to poor old Todd," she whispered. "But you're too late, honey."

She put her letter to Todd in the basket and removed Elizabeth's. Feeling doubly satisfied, she walked away, tapping the elegant blue envelope against her palm. *Get ready to be dumped, wonder twin!* she thought.

As she turned to go, Maria breezed in with some letters to mail. "Hey, Nicole, how's it going?" she said as she dropped her mail in the basket.

"Great," Nicole answered. "I'm having a great day."

Maria glanced at the blue envelope that Nicole was holding. "Oh, yeah? Then why are you walking away from the mailbox with that letter still in your hand?"

"Oh, this is nothing," Nicole said, moving to tuck the envelope into the pocket of her shorts.

Maria stopped her. "Isn't that Elizabeth's new stationery?"

"Yeah." Nicole shrugged, forcing herself not to appear guilty. "Elizabeth let me borrow it. Isn't she sweet?"

Maria's eyes narrowed. "And you don't mind that it's inscribed with her initial?"

Nicole laughed nervously. "Beggars can't be choosers, right?"

Maria shook her head. "I don't think so. Come here." She took Nicole's arm and practically dragged her to a chair in the corner. "Sit down," Maria commanded, her eyes brimming with suspicion. Caught off guard, Nicole obeyed.

"OK," Maria said, standing over her, "tell me the truth." Nicole lowered her eyes. "I don't know what you mean."

"I think there's something fishy going on," Maria said. "Let me see that letter."

"It's nothing." Nicole started to get up, but Maria pushed her back into the chair.

"The letter, Nicole." Maria held out her hand. "Give it to me."

Nicole hesitated, trying to think of an excuse. *What's the use?* she thought. Maria already hated her for stealing Elizabeth's play. Without a word, Nicole handed over the letter.

"I don't understand you, Nicole. This letter is from Elizabeth, addressed to Todd. Why did you take it?" Maria demanded.

Nicole raised her chin defiantly. "Because Elizabeth Wakefield is a dirty, rotten cheat. She's stringing Todd along while she's kissing up to Joey. It makes me sick!"

Maria raised her eyebrows. "And instead of

minding your own business, you've decided to steal from the U.S. mail? That's low, Nicole. Even for you. Plus, it's a felony."

"This *is* my business," Nicole shot back. "You know how much I was looking forward to seeing Joey this summer. Elizabeth ruined everything."

"I know how you feel," Maria said, her voice dripping with sweetness, as if she were playing the role of Understanding Friend in a TV movie.

Nicole glared at her. "Don't give me that acting-school empathy. You don't know how I feel at all! I hate Elizabeth Wakefield." She said it again, louder.

Maria shook her head. "You don't mean that."

"Oh, yes, I do," Nicole shouted. "I hate her stinking guts. Dizzy Lizzie deserves to rot in a ditch. My whole life is torn apart because of her, and she's getting away with cheating on her boyfriend—with *my* boyfriend!" She felt a sob rip through her. "And Elizabeth Wakefield stole the best friend I ever had! I hate her so much, I wish she would just die."

Maria stood back, gawking at her.

Nicole inhaled a deep, shaky breath. "I know when you move back to Sweet Valley, you'll forget all about me."

Maria placed her hand on Nicole's shoulder. "That's not true," she said softly.

Nicole shrugged her away. "Don't lie to me, Maria.

You've been going on about Elizabeth Wakefield and Sweet Valley ever since I've known you."

Maria sighed. "We need to talk." She pulled up another chair and sat facing Nicole. "Yes, it's true that I'm happy to be returning to Sweet Valley," she admitted. "I moved there during a difficult time in my life, when I believed myself to be a Hollywood has-been at the age of twelve. Sweet Valley was the first place I'd ever lived where I could simply be me—Maria Slater, regular girl.

"But I also have wonderful memories of New York and the fun times we've had." She shook Nicole's shoulder. "Remember the time we rode the train into the city and got lost trying to find Tower Records on Broadway?"

Nicole smiled reluctantly. "I still don't know how we ended up in New Jersey."

"How could I forget all that?" Maria asked. "Or the day we met, when you stood up in American lit class and told those creeps to shut up."

Nicole remembered that, too. They'd been discussing a novel by Zora Neale Hurston when a couple of overgrown Neanderthals began making racist slurs, aiming them at the only black student in the class—Maria. Nicole had been furious and hadn't hesitated to let them know. After that, she and Maria had become fast friends, and for the first time in her life, Nicole hadn't felt lonely.

"It's scary to think of going home and not having you there," she said.

Maria's expression softened. "If you'd treat people better, you'd have lots of friends."

Nicole shrugged. "I don't know about that. I've never been very popular."

"And if you'd quit feeling sorry for yourself . . ." Maria chuckled. "The jig is up, Nicole. I *know* there's a nice person trapped inside all that bad attitude."

Nicole wrinkled her nose. "Cute, Maria." Then, in spite of herself, she started to laugh.

Maria hugged her. "I *will* miss you, Nicole. I don't know when we'll see each other again, but I promise to be a faithful pen pal."

"I guess that'll have to do," Nicole said. Then she remembered her letter to Todd. In a small town like Sweet Valley, it wouldn't take long for everyone to know what she'd done. She took a deep breath and let it out slowly. "There's something else. Another letter."

Maria frowned. "What other letter?"

"I wrote to Todd this afternoon. And, well . . . I included a snapshot of Elizabeth and Joey."

Maria jumped out of her chair. "Come on," she ordered, dragging Nicole back to the mail basket.

Under Maria's watchful eye, Nicole removed the letter she'd written to Todd and replaced the one from Elizabeth. Then she handed her letter to Maria, who ripped it into shreds.

"Don't you feel better now?" Maria asked.

Nicole shrugged. In a way, it was nice to have everything out in the open between her and Maria. But on the other hand, it would have been great fun to mess up Elizabeth's life.

Maria seemed to be waiting for an answer. Nicole sighed. "OK, I'll try. I don't like Elizabeth and I probably never will, but I promise I'll stop the out-and-out tricks. I'm still looking forward to beating her to a pulp in the color war, though."

Maria hugged her again. "That's all I'm asking for. And of course we're going to beat them on Saturday. Red team rules!"

As they left the camp office Nicole's mind drifted to the upcoming color war. She was going to have to beat Elizabeth without any dirty play. *Thank goodness I switched Joey to my team before I made that promise,* she thought. *By the time the color war is over, he will be mine.*

Chapter 8

Early Saturday morning a strange noise outside the cabin woke Jessica. Instantly alert, she opened her eyes. *Paul!* her mind shouted. *At last!*

Although she was normally a late riser, and a slow one at that, she bolted out of bed in less than a heartbeat and got dressed. Her whole body tingled with anticipation as she opened the door. "I don't believe it," she groaned. Instead of seeing Paul's gorgeous face, as she'd expected, Jessica found herself staring at a scene that was straight out of a hokey credit card commercial.

Lila and Bo were sitting at a picnic table under a tree, toasting each other with crystal goblets of orange juice. The table was draped with a white lace tablecloth. Covered silver serving dishes and wicker baskets of fresh fruit and rolls were arranged around a centerpiece of fresh flowers. A beam of early-morning sunlight reflected off the rim of a delicate gold-rimmed china plate.

Two waiters in starched white uniforms stood at attention at either end of the table. Recognizing Buford and Johansen, Jessica stifled a giggle. *Now I've seen everything,* she thought. Shaking her head, she closed the door and headed back to bed.

After breakfast the counselors and campers gathered at the large field behind the main lodge for the official start of the color war. The day was sunny but not too warm, and the air was alive with the buzz of excited chatter. Nicole smiled, thinking of how she'd stolen Joey away from Elizabeth's team. *That was just for starters,* she thought. She planned on stealing him, period, by the end of the day.

Lacey marched into the center, banging her metal pot with a wooden spoon. "Attention, everyone. Will our two captains please step forward?"

Nicole and Elizabeth walked to the center of the group and faced each other. Nicole glared into Elizabeth's eyes. Elizabeth lifted her chin a notch and held Nicole's gaze, meeting the silent challenge. *You're done for, wonder twin, but you're too stupid to know it,* Nicole thought, grinning.

"OK, girls," Lacey said. "Shake hands, and may the best team win."

Nicole gave Elizabeth's hand an extrahard squeeze. *Get ready for the beating of your pathetic life, Dizzy Lizzie,* she thought.

Lacey banged on the pot again. "As I call your names, please line up behind your captain." When she got to Winston Egbert's name, she said, "Red team."

"But I'm on the blue team," he protested. "Look at me—I'm even wearing blue socks."

Lacey gave him a pointed look, then continued reading names. Nicole held her breath when Lacey reached the *M*'s. ". . . Joey Mason, blue team . . ."

Nicole blanched, her feet rooted to the ground.

"Wait a minute, Lacey," Joey interrupted. "I thought I was on the red team."

"Hey, Joey, you want my socks?" Winston asked.

Lacey glanced up with a look of impatience. "This is the official list. You boys will have to go back to your cabins and change to avoid confusion."

Joey chuckled and raised his hands in surrender. "Hey, I'm not complaining." He jogged over to Elizabeth's side, giving her a huge grin.

Nicole's hands clenched into tight fists. *What happened?* she wondered. Either she'd fixed the wrong lists, or Lacey had caught the change and switched Winston and Joey back to their original teams.

Her blue-green eyes filled with fury and her prissy pink lips twisted into a smug little smile, Elizabeth glared at Nicole.

Nicole raised her chin defiantly. *You may have won this time, Dizzy Lizzie, but don't get used to it,* Nicole thought. *It won't happen again.*

Jessica whooped with delight as she passed Maria in the speed-walk relay. Pumping her arms, she pushed herself to go faster, widening the gap between them.

The next person up for the blue team was Johansen. He flashed Jessica a metallic smile, his braces glinting as she handed him the team's baton, a short wooden stick that was painted blue.

Taking a deep breath, Jessica ambled over to a grassy spot. She wasn't wearing a watch, but she guessed that it was nearly noon. *Paul should have been here by now,* she thought.

Sarah, Stephanie, and Tanya, the Wanna-bes on the blue team, ran over to join her. Tanya and Sarah grabbed the spots on either side of Jessica. Stephanie stuck out her bottom lip, her green eyes turning moist. "I want to thit next to Jessica, too."

Jessica patted the ground in front of her. "Right here."

Stephanie gave her a big, gap-toothed grin and plopped herself down. A second later, her legs were in the air and she was doing scissor kicks, which Jessica had taught them in dance class. Jessica shook her head, marveling at the kid's energy.

All the Wanna-bes were wearing their hair up that day because they wanted to look like Jessica. *And I wanted to look like Elizabeth,* Jessica thought with a laugh. *But my wonderful plan won't matter if Paul can't see me today.*

"You were so fast in the race, Jessica," Sarah said, her dark, almond-shaped eyes filled with adoration.

"Yeah, you were fast as a bullet," Tanya said.

"I think you were faster than an eagle," Stephanie grunted, still scissor-kicking.

Jessica laughed in spite of her frustration over Paul. *I have to call him,* she thought. *That's all there is to it.* She jumped to her feet, and her three little shadows did the same. "I have to go do something—by myself," she said. "And I was hoping you guys would save my seat. It's so nice and shady in this spot."

Tanya gave her a wary look. "Are you coming back in just a few minutes?"

"In only *one* minute," Jessica promised. To her

99

relief, they bought it. Careful to avoid being seen by Lacey, Jessica stole away to the main lodge to call Paul.

Her conversation with Paul lasted barely a minute, but Jessica hung up completely satisfied. *He's on his way!* she cheered silently. Finally she and Paul would be together.

Now all she had to do was find her twin—and persuade Liz to go along with her brilliant plan.

Later that day, as the wheelbarrow race reached its exciting conclusion, Jessica's Wannabes—both blue and red—jumped up and down on the sidelines, cheering frantically. "Go, Jessica! Go, Jessica!"

But it was Elizabeth who was suffering from scraped palms and strained shoulders as she walked her hands in a jerky path toward the finish line. Her back felt as if it were ready to break. Her partner, thirteen-year-old Tiffany, smacked Elizabeth's feet together and screamed for her to go faster.

Elizabeth winced as her left hand landed on a sharp pebble. *I'll get you for this, Jessica!* she vowed.

Her sister had left camp shortly after lunch to meet Paul, leaving Elizabeth to do double duty for their team. "Just for a little while," Jessica had pleaded. And Elizabeth had reluctantly agreed. *Just like I always do,* she thought hotly.

"Faster, Jessica!" Tiffany shouted.

From the corner of her eye, Elizabeth caught a glimpse of Nancy and Angela, the red team's "wheelbarrow," inching ahead of her. Steeling herself, Elizabeth picked up speed, a deep groan escaping her lips.

But despite Elizabeth's effort, Angela and Nancy stayed in the lead all the way to the finish line. Ignoring Tiffany's snooty look of accusation, Elizabeth staggered to a shady spot under a tree and plopped down on the ground.

Maria came over to her with two paper cups of cold lemonade. "That was a valiant effort, Jess," she said, offering Elizabeth one of the cups.

Elizabeth took it and gulped the lemonade down eagerly. "I'm going to kill her."

Maria frowned. "That's not very sporting of you. Angela and Nancy won fair and square. Besides, it's only a game, and your team is still ahead by two points."

Elizabeth crumpled the paper cup in her fist. "I can't believe she did this to me again."

Maria leaned back, her eyes wide with astonishment. "You're *Liz!*" She pursed her lips and folded her arms. "OK, what's going on?" she asked, nailing Elizabeth with a no-nonsense look.

"Jessica—what else?" Elizabeth shook her head and sighed deeply. "It's hard enough being me. Having to be her, too, is killing me. I've had to enter twice as many events so that Lacey won't get suspicious." She leaned back against the tree and closed her eyes.

"Where is she?" Maria asked.

Elizabeth opened her eyes. "Gone. She left a few hours ago to meet Paul."

Maria leaned back against the tree next to Elizabeth. "Still the same old Jessica, I see. Remember the time back in seventh grade when she and Lila stole the principal's toupee?"

Elizabeth smiled, too worn out to laugh.

"I don't know why you keep covering for her," Maria said.

"I don't either," Elizabeth replied honestly. She glanced at her watch and groaned. It was four o'clock, time for her next event. Reluctantly she dragged herself to her feet. "I get to be Elizabeth now," she said.

"Are you going to be all right?" Maria asked. "You look exhausted. I hope you didn't sign up for the rope-climbing contest."

"No way," Elizabeth said, brushing the dry pine needles off the seat of her khaki shorts. "I knew I'd be tired out by now, so I picked the egg toss."

Maria looked up at her with a doubtful expression.

"I was galloping on my bare hands just a few minutes ago," Elizabeth reminded her. "The egg toss is going to be the easiest thing I've done all day."

The egg toss was being held in the area between the nature cabin and the main lodge. When Elizabeth arrived, the teams were starting to line up under Rose's direction. Elizabeth groaned when she saw Nicole talking to some of the red players. Her red baseball cap, worn backward, bobbed up and down as she nodded. *Why do I always get stuck having to do battle with her?* Elizabeth wondered. *I guess we're just fated to be enemies.*

Rose called for attention and began to explain the rules. The object of the game was to pass a raw egg down the line, tossing the egg from person to person with a spoon. The teams scored ten points for each egg that made it to the end of the line and one point for each egg the other team dropped.

Elizabeth felt a warm touch on her shoulder. She turned and saw Joey standing behind her. A wonderful feeling of joy shot through her. She smiled at him, and he winked. Elizabeth suddenly realized she wasn't tired anymore. *Seeing him is better than eating a truckload of vitamins,* she thought.

When Elizabeth turned around, she noticed Nicole watching her with a hateful look in her eyes. *She must have seen Joey winking at me,* Elizabeth realized. Refusing to be intimidated, she glared right back at Nicole.

After Rose had passed out the spoons, she called for the action to start. Everyone began to cheer as the eggs made their way from spoon to spoon. In line ahead of Elizabeth, Tanya caught an egg with remarkable skill.

Elizabeth felt a surge of competitive spirit. *I never knew I had it in me, but I want to win so badly that I can taste it,* she thought as she held her spoon steady for Tanya's toss. Suddenly, out of the corner of her eye, Elizabeth saw Nicole fling her arm up, shooting an egg into the air. And with a firm-sounding crack, it landed right on Elizabeth's head.

Elizabeth gasped. All around her, everyone was clapping and laughing as the glob of sticky egg dripped down her forehead, into her eyes, over her nose and lips. Rose stopped laughing long enough to announce, "Blue team's point"—which made everyone laugh even harder.

Elizabeth's face burned with humiliation, and hot tears filled her eyes. Even Joey was laughing.

Feeling utterly alone and abandoned, she covered her face and ran.

In the privacy of the girls' room in the main lodge, Elizabeth leaned against one of the sinks and sobbed. Her mind kept replaying the memory of Joey laughing at her. Suddenly another picture flashed in her head—the image of how Nicole was probably gloating over her victory at that very moment.

"She hasn't beaten me yet," Elizabeth said aloud with renewed determination. She yanked a fistful of paper towels from the wall dispenser and turned on the faucet. "Now, what's the fastest way to rinse this gooey mess out of my hair?" she asked her reflection.

"How's our friend Phil doing?" Jessica asked. She and Paul were lounging over a late picnic lunch of thick ham sandwiches on potato bread, with chocolate chip cookies for dessert. They'd spent the afternoon hiking on Echo Mountain and had stopped to eat in a beautiful spot next to a waterfall. The crashing sound of the powerful stream reminded her of the waves breaking on the shore back home.

Jessica lay back on the checkered tablecloth, tucking her hands under her head. Paul had told her that this was his favorite place in the whole world.

He stretched out next to her. "As far as I know, Phil is doing just fine."

"He sure saved my neck the other night," she said.

Paul propped himself up on his elbow and leaned over her. "Phil is a filly, Jessica. *She* saved your neck."

She giggled. "I didn't know. Anyway, I'd love to take *her* riding again sometime."

They both laughed. Then his expression became serious. "I never thought I'd meet anyone like you," he said softly. "This must be my lucky summer."

Jessica pulled him down and kissed him. "I'm lucky, too. I sure didn't expect the summer to turn out the way it has."

He kissed her again. "I just hope you don't get into trouble because of me."

"I don't think anyone is going to miss me," she said flippantly. "With the frenzy over the color war, they wouldn't even notice if Crazy Freddy walked into camp."

"Poor Crazy Freddy. It's so hard for him to make friends," Paul joked.

Jessica laughed. "That's because he chops them to bits."

"That's just his way of saying 'howdy,'" Paul said as he reached for another cookie.

Jessica sat up and hugged her knees. "I'd have to teach him how to be cool," she said, giggling.

Paul scowled at her, as if he were jealous. "Oh, sure, now that you've got me, you're all eager to move on to another challenge."

"How'd you guess?" she said with a laugh. "But even if we did get him to hang out with us and be part of the color war, he'd probably insist on joining Nicole's team."

"Why?" Paul asked.

Jessica giggled. "Because red is his favorite color—*blood* red, to be precise."

Paul wrinkled his noise. "That was bad, Jessica."

She laid her hand on his arm. "Oh, but wouldn't it be wild if he really did show up this summer? What do you think Lacey would do?"

He sat up, sucked in his upper lip, and narrowed his eyes. "Attention, please," he drawled, mimicking Lacey's southern accent. He grabbed the top off one of the picnic containers and banged on it with a plastic spoon. "Attention! You with the bloody ax . . . yes, young man, I'm talking to you! We don't allow carousing at this fine, upstanding camp. . . . Don't you growl at me. You just put that bloody ax down and march yourself right out of here! Quit waving that ax in my face, young man. By the way, can you cook? It's been a long time since Camp Echo Mountain has seen an edible meal."

Jessica was doubled over with laughter. "*That* would be worth seeing." A crazy idea popped into her head. She reached for another cookie and chewed it thoughtfully. "Hey, Paul, you want to have some fun?" she asked, flashing him a diabolical grin.

Chapter 9

Dinner was served outside in the main picnic area that evening. When Lacey announced the scores from the day's events, a cheer rose from the cluster of tables where the blue team was sitting—they were ahead by three points. "It's not over yet," Lacey said. "After dinner we'll have our final contest, capture the flag, which is worth ten points."

Everyone seemed to be in high spirits, calling out "Blue is best" and "Red team rules." Elizabeth tried to appear enthusiastic, but inside she was frantic because Jessica still hadn't returned.

Maria stopped by her table, looking out of place in her red T-shirt. A few of the blue team's members booed and hissed. She laughed good-naturedly and turned to Elizabeth. "Is she back yet?" she asked in a whisper.

"No," Elizabeth answered glumly. She scooped up a forkful of stringy meat slathered with barbecue sauce, then set it back on her tray. "What is this stuff? Beef? Pork?"

Maria scrunched up her nose. "I was wondering the same thing myself. It could be roadkill, for all I know."

"I don't think I'm very hungry," Elizabeth said, pushing her tray away.

"Bernard is hopeless," Maria said with a laugh. "But try the beans, Liz. They aren't too bad."

Elizabeth shook her head. "My stomach feels like it's tied up in a big knot. I tried to find Lila earlier, to see if she knew where Jessica was planning to go."

Maria's eyes narrowed. "I haven't seen Lila all day, come to think of it. Where do you suppose she's escaped to?"

Elizabeth shrugged. "Who knows? I haven't seen Bo either. Maybe they're all having a great time on a double date while I'm stuck here playing Jessica." She glanced at her watch and sighed. "Jess volunteered to help set up for capture the flag, so I guess I'd better go do that."

"See you later, *Jessica*," Maria said with a sly smile.

Elizabeth rolled her eyes. As she headed toward the main field, Joey came up behind her and pulled her behind a tree. "Jessica, huh?" he whispered close to her ear. "I don't think so."

Elizabeth smiled, glowing with the pleasure of running into Joey unexpectedly. "I'm still amazed that you can tell us apart," she said, gazing into his deep green eyes.

Joey kissed her, then took her hand in his. "Let's go for a walk. I've wanted to be alone with you all day."

"I can't," she said wistfully. "I have to cover for Jess—" Elizabeth stopped in midsentence, realizing what she was saying. *I'm supposed to be playing Jessica,* she thought with a smile. *I might as well enjoy myself as much as she does.* "Sure, I can go for a walk with you," she told Joey.

"That was a sudden change of mind," Joey commented.

"I'm just letting myself get into the character," Elizabeth replied. "Isn't that what acting is all about? Jessica would never let her chores stop her from sneaking off with a gorgeous guy."

He laughed. "That makes perfect sense. And thanks for the compliment. I think you're gorgeous, too."

Elizabeth sighed, happy and contented as she and Joey headed toward the boathouse at a leisurely pace. The sun was beginning to set, casting bright colors over the lake. In the eastern sky, a full moon was rising.

When they reached the boathouse, Joey took her into his arms and cleared his throat. "I'm sorry about what happened during the egg toss."

Elizabeth shrugged, pushing away the humiliating memory. "I suppose it did look funny."

"I didn't realize how hurt you were until it was too late." He brought her hand to his lips and kissed it. "I'm sure it wasn't an accident. Nicole hit you on purpose. I feel like such a heel for laughing at you."

"It happened and it's over," Elizabeth said. "I don't want to talk about it."

Joey nodded and pulled her into his arms. "I'm on your side forever," he whispered. "You know that, don't you?"

She tilted her head and looked into his emerald green eyes. The tension of the day seemed to drain away as she stood in the warm circle of his arms. The woods were cool and dark, the pungent fragrance of pine lingering in the air. Elizabeth's whole body tingled as Joey lowered his lips to hers.

Suddenly his hands became tense. She blinked, then froze. There it was again—the sound of somebody chopping wood.

Joey cursed. "I'm going to stop that girl once and for all." He was about to charge into the forest, but Elizabeth pulled him back.

"Don't go after her," she pleaded. "It's exactly what Nicole wants. You'll just be encouraging her little game by paying attention to her."

Joey's jaw tightened. "I suppose you're right. I just wish she would find someone else to torment."

Elizabeth closed her eyes and silently wished the same thing. Sadly she realized the romantic mood had been shattered. *Thanks a lot, Nicole!* she thought. "I'm more determined than ever to win this color war," she told Joey.

He squeezed her hand. "Then that's what we'll do, captain!"

When they returned to the main field, Joey stopped in his tracks and frowned. Elizabeth looked and saw that Nicole was sitting on a picnic table surrounded by her admirers from the red team. "How did she get back here so fast?" he asked.

Elizabeth felt a cold, tingling sensation in the back of her neck, as if someone were watching her. She turned quickly, but the only people behind her were campers and counselors. No one seemed to be staring at her.

Something's not right, she thought. *In fact, I have a feeling that something is terribly, terribly wrong.*

Jessica snuggled closer to Paul in the cab of his faded red pickup truck, which was parked along the unpaved service road near the camp. They were sharing the last can of root beer from their picnic as they waited for the sun to set.

"What do you get when you cross an ax murderer with a fisherman?" Paul asked.

Jessica paused as she raised the drink to her lips. "I don't know. What?"

"A never-ending supply of sushi," Paul answered.

They both doubled over with laughter. Then Paul said, "It wasn't all that funny, Jess," which made her laugh so hard that she dropped the root beer, splashing the seat cover and his jeans.

"Charming," he said, his eyes sparkling with humor as he groped under the seat for something to wipe up the spill. He found an old green sock and shrugged. "This will do."

Jessica giggled, and Paul eyed her with a stern glare. "You'd better not be laughing at my all-purpose cleaning tool," he warned.

"What if I am?" she taunted. "How are you going to stop me?"

"This, I'll have you know . . ." Paul held up the soggy sock. "Is a precision instrument."

Jessica grabbed it away and tossed it on his head. "Not to mention a fashion accessory."

He yanked it off and scowled at her. Then they fell together in peals of hysterical laughter. "You're completely out of control, Jessica," he said. "Are you sure you want to go through with this?"

She leaned back and looked at him directly. "Don't tell me you're wimping out on me," she teased.

Paul raised his eyebrows. "Who, me? Not a chance. But come on, Jessica, sneaking into camp and scaring everyone? Won't you get into big trouble with Lacey?"

She shook her head. "Don't worry. Lacey's the one who told us the ghost story in the first place. I'm sure she'll enjoy a good scare."

"If you say so." He looked through the windshield at the sky. "We may as well go now. It'll be completely dark by the time we hike to the camp."

Jessica clapped her hands together. "OK, let's get this party started."

"You're sure?" he asked again.

"Let's go!" she cried, pushing open the door.

Paul grabbed the props they'd gathered for their prank from the back of the truck.

"Do you have everything?" Jessica asked.

"Let's see." Paul held up each item as he ran through the list. "Old hubcap for me to bang on trees, flashlights, leftover ham sandwich in case I get hungry, your sponge-on-a-stick . . . I don't know, Jessica. Do you really think you'll fool anyone with that?" he asked. Jessica had created an "ax" from a tree branch and an old sponge she'd found in Paul's truck.

"Sure it will," she replied, wielding the flimsy prop as if it were a real ax. "It'll be dark, and all anyone will see is a shadow. That's what acting is all about—creating illusions. I learned that from Joey when I was rehearsing for *Lakeside Love.*"

Paul gave her a doubtful look. "OK, but if it doesn't work, they'll all think that Crazy Freddy came down from the mountain to give everyone a bath."

Jessica laughed and gave him a playful shove. "The discussion is over. Let's hit the trail."

"Whatever you say, boss."

"That's better," Jessica quipped, giddy with anticipation.

"We're ahead by only three points," Elizabeth said. She and her team were in a huddle behind the main lodge, planning their strategy. The excitement of the day had reached a fever pitch, and now, with Joey sitting across from her, Elizabeth felt as if she were on top of the world. "The ten points from capture the flag will determine the winning team."

"We have to beat them," Jennifer declared as she chewed on a clump of her red hair. Her chin was covered with a film of dried barbecue sauce.

Elizabeth winced out of habit, then realized she really didn't care about Jennifer's messy habits anymore. *It seems I can get used to anything*, Elizabeth thought.

"Yeah, we have to beat those red creeps," Bryan yelled. He was the smallest ten-year-old boy at camp, but his loud, booming voice made up for his size.

A few others chimed in until everyone was chanting, "Beat the red! Beat the red!"

"Does everyone understand how to play?" Elizabeth asked. "We each get a bandanna and tuck it into our waistbands, and then if someone takes it away, you have to sit out the rest of the game in their prison—unless one of us manages to rescue you."

Odette, the only thirteen-year-old at camp who didn't have a bad attitude, raised her hand. "I have a suggestion. How about if each of the older kids watches out for one of the little kids?"

"That's a good idea," Elizabeth said, impressed.

Tiffany, the blond leader of the Sulky Six, spoke up enthusiastically. "And when the red players come after our rug rats, the older kids can steal their red flag."

Stephanie, her younger sister, stuck out her lip. "'Rug rats' isn't a very nice name, Tiffany."

"Yeah," Tanya agreed. "I'm going to tell Jessica that you called us that."

At the mention of her wayward sister, Elizabeth's jaw clenched. If she hadn't been so angry, she'd have been worried sick. What was supposed to have been a switch for an hour or so had already stretched past sunset.

The Wanna-bes had come to her earlier that afternoon, whining for Jessica and demanding to know where she'd gone. Elizabeth had told them that Jessica was working on a big surprise for them. *Let her figure a way out of that one!* Elizabeth thought with satisfaction.

Lacey's voice sounded over the loudspeaker, calling the teams back to the main field. Before the group broke apart, Joey raised his hands. "What's the best team of all time?"

The others shouted back, "Blue team!"

"Who's going to win?" Elizabeth asked, pushing Jessica out of her mind and getting into the spirit of the game.

"Blue team! Hooray!"

As they headed over to the field, Nicole sauntered up to Elizabeth. "How's my favorite loser?" she said derisively.

Elizabeth ignored her and kept walking. Nicole fell into step beside her. *Can't she take a hint?* Elizabeth thought hotly. Nicole adjusted her red baseball cap. "This is it, I guess—what we've all been waiting for. Prepare to die, Dizzy Lizzie.

118

I'm planning to capture the flag—and Joey."

Elizabeth stopped, her fists clenched as she turned to Nicole. The sight of her smug expression filled Elizabeth with red-hot anger.

Nicole raised her eyebrows, glowering. "What are you going to do, wonder twin? Punch me out with those dainty little hands of yours? Gee, I'm really scared."

"What is your *problem*?" Elizabeth demanded.

Nicole flashed her a wide, cold grin. "You." And with that, she turned to go.

"Nicole Banes, you are such a . . . a . . ." Elizabeth sputtered, so angry she could barely speak. A hundred nasty retorts filled her mind, but her voice seemed to disappear. Right then she wished she had some of Jessica's ability to be venomous—she would have loved to say something brutal.

Someone stepped outside an old abandoned cabin deep in the woods. The moon was full, and the ax was waiting by the door. Taking a deep breath of crisp evening air, the person smiled in appreciation. The forest was filled with life. But to sustain life, there also had to be death. It was the decaying leaves that nourished the soil, the swamp that sheltered the breeding creatures. This was the cycle of life. The forest—the entire planet—required death to stay alive. Those who chose to use the forest had to be willing to pay its price.

Visions of long blond hair danced through the person's mind. What would it look like, stained with blood, spread across the forest floor?

The person picked up the ax and grinned. The worn wooden handle felt like an old friend—a best friend. Filled with anticipation, the person ran a finger along the sharp blade and thought, *Tonight will be a night to remember.*

The cycle of life had to continue. The forest demanded its due.

Chapter 10

Jessica's foot slipped, leaving her dangling from a high branch of a maple tree. "I'm going to fall," she shrieked.

Climbing behind her, Paul snorted. "That'll help keep our hiding place a secret." His strong hands grasped her by the waist and boosted her up to the next branch. He pulled himself up beside her.

Jessica gave him a sideways grin. "I can't believe I let you talk me into this," she said. He glared at her incredulously. Jessica giggled.

"OK, enough fooling around," she said, forcing herself to get serious. Crouched together in the tree, she and Paul could see the field and most of the main area of the camp, where everyone was running around playing capture the flag.

Jessica pointed out the location of each team's

prison in the woods near the edge of the camp, where players who lost their flags would have to go. "Stay clear of that whole area," she told him. "Someone might see you."

"I don't know about this," Paul said.

She leaned closer and kissed him. "It'll be great. Just remember to stay out of sight. We don't want you getting arrested for trespassing."

Paul rolled his eyes. Jessica dissolved in a fit of giddy laughter.

Elizabeth panted as she chased Winston across the field and into the picnic area. He leaped on top of a picnic table, his footsteps thumping as he ran across the wooden planks and jumped off the other end.

Elizabeth darted around the table, then ran after him as he headed toward the main buildings. As they neared the drama cabin she finally caught him. She grabbed his flag and let out a cry of joy.

Then Winston tripped over an exposed tree root, and she fell on top of him.

"OK, OK, I'm yours," he said, laughing and gasping for breath. "But Nicole is going to kill me for losing that flag. Maybe I could buy it back from you, Liz? I'll give you some of my jalapeño jelly beans."

Elizabeth waved the red bandanna in the air. "Forget it, buddy. This is war."

"And my fern and moss collection?" he squeaked.

She stood up and nudged him with the toe of her shoe. "On your feet, boy! We're going to prison."

"Have you no mercy?" he wailed.

Laughing, Elizabeth shoved him onward. "None at all. Now move it!"

He placed his hands on top of his head, as if he were being held at gunpoint, and marched ahead of her.

The team prisons were located a few yards apart from each other, in a densely wooded spot near the edge of the camp. A clear, wide path led to the area, but Elizabeth felt as if she and Winston were wandering deep into the wilderness. The trees seemed to loom over them, casting long, threatening shadows in the fading light.

"What if I were to throw in half a package of pecan cookies?" Winston pleaded over his shoulder. "They're hardly stale."

Elizabeth was about to tell Winston to give it up when she was suddenly startled by the sound of a twig snapping nearby. Her whole body tightened, and a whisper of terror ran through her. Again she felt a tingling sensation in the back of her neck, as if she were being watched.

"Are you considering those cookies?" Winston asked.

Elizabeth blinked, shaking herself alert. Winston wasn't acting as though he'd heard anything strange. *It was probably a player running through the woods,* she assured herself.

She pushed aside her fear and scowled at her prisoner. "No way, Winston. I'll never take a bribe!"

"I've got you now," Nicole yelled as she chased after Joey. He looked like a wild stallion, running with power and grace, the blue bandanna flapping at his side. There was no way she'd let him get away from her.

They headed toward the lake, jumping over rocks and tree roots in their path. Nicole could hardly breathe, and her leg muscles burned. Finally she caught up to him and leaped forward, grabbing his flag. Hooting with delight, she waved the blue fabric in the air. "Red team rules!"

Joey was lying on the ground, panting. His light brown hair, messy and damp with sweat, hung over his eyes. His muscular arms were glistening. He was gorgeous.

Nicole stood over him, admiring her prize. "I guess you and I have a date," she said. "Come along, Joey. Red prison awaits."

"OK, Nicole, you have my flag. There's no need to gloat."

"I'm sorry," she said. "It's just that you're Camp Echo Mountain's best catch."

The corners of his lips turned up in a smirking grin. "Those are the breaks, I guess." He slowly rose to his feet.

Nicole looped her arm through his and flashed him a big smile. *What a fabulous day!* she thought. She was almost certain the red team was winning. And now she had Joey in her power—at least until the end of the game.

He wasn't scowling at her, as he had been lately. That was a hopeful sign. Maybe she still had a chance with him. After all, the wonder twin would be going back to Todd in a few days. That would leave Joey with a broken heart—and Nicole to help him mend it on the trip back to New York.

As she led Joey through the woods, Nicole spotted Elizabeth and Winston a few yards ahead on the path.

Nicole grinned mischievously. "Oh, Joey, you're such a prize," she said, loud enough for Elizabeth to overhear. "And you're all mine. I think I'll stay and guard you myself. The red team can win this game without me."

She glanced at Elizabeth. The wonder twin was glaring at them with her face twisted into a big, ugly scowl. Nicole laughed, feeling as though she had just conquered an entire army all by herself.

Jessica jumped to the ground, followed by Paul. "OK, this is it," she whispered. "I'll stand on this side and make ghost noises while you sneak around to the other side and bang on trees."

Paul cupped his hands around her face. "I think you're a bad influence on me, Jess. You've got me doing crazy things."

Jessica giggled. "Crazy is good, Paul." She reached up and kissed him firmly on the lips. "That's for luck," she whispered. "Now go."

She waved to him with her make-believe ax and watched him disappear into the dark woods. The temperature had dropped considerably after sunset, raising gooseflesh on her legs and arms. Jessica wished she had thought to borrow one of the sweaters Paul kept in his truck.

She rubbed her arms briskly, trying to warm her skin as she waited in the shadows. After he had been gone a few minutes, she decided the time had come for her to make her entrance. Ducking from tree to tree, she crept closer to the main field. With everyone running around and hollering, no one seemed to notice Jessica as she crouched behind a fat oak tree.

Maria and Tad Winslow came charging after each other just a few feet from Jessica's hiding place. She held her breath, then exhaled as they darted off toward the lake.

Jessica let out a nervous laugh. "It's show time," she whispered. She cupped her hands around her mouth and let out a deep, eerie moan. A few players stopped running and began to shuffle around anxiously.

Enjoying herself immensely, Jessica raised the stick-and-sponge ax and moaned again. Suddenly a strong arm hooked around her throat, causing her to let go of the stick.

She laughed and crossed her arms. "Very funny, Paul. Now go bang that hubcap like you're supposed to and leave me to do my job." She tried to turn around to face him, but the hold around her neck was too tight.

"Hey, stop it," she said, irritated. "Didn't we agree you'd never—"

The arm squeezed against her throat, cutting off her air. *He's not joking,* she realized. A cold, sinking feeling of terror came over her.

Then the voice of a stranger, low and hoarse, spoke into her ear. "Come, blondie. The forest needs you."

Jessica opened her mouth to scream, but only a hollow, gasping sound emerged. Her lungs burned as she struggled to take in a breath.

She fought desperately, thrashing about and digging her fingernails into his arm. Despite her efforts, he continued to pull her backward into the woods.

A numbing haze seemed to fall over her, dragging her down to soothing nothingness. Jessica knew what it meant: She was suffocating and would soon lose consciousness. Her mind throbbed with panic, forcing her to keep fighting.

She heard a small voice scream her name. At first she thought she'd imagined it. Then she saw Tanya pop out from behind a tree, her dark brown eyes wide with fear.

Jessica tried to wave her away, but Tanya rushed forward, yelling, "Let Jessica go!"

The man stopped. Using his free arm, he punched Tanya, his fist striking her face with a loud smack. She fell heavily to the ground.

Jessica stared in horror, transfixed by the sight of Tanya's small body lying very still, facedown in the dirt. The stylish chignon Jessica had arranged her hair in that morning was pulled askew, and her short blue socks were covered in mud.

Jessica squeezed her eyes shut, tears spilling down her face. A thick cloud of despair swirled around her as she continued to sink deeper into oblivion.

To her surprise, the man suddenly loosened

his strangling hold around her neck. Jessica doubled over and gasped, filling her lungs. Her relief was short-lived. He grabbed a fistful of her long hair and wrapped it around his hand like a leash. "Not a sound, blondie," he warned. He yanked hard, jerking her head back. A bolt of pain shot through her.

Still holding Jessica's hair, he bent down and grabbed Tanya by the back of her blue shirt. He swung her small body over his shoulder as if she were nothing more than a sack of potatoes.

He tugged on Jessica's hair, forcing her to look directly into his face. His forehead was marked with an angry red scar, and his nose was crooked, as if it had been broken in a few places. With a scraggly dark beard covering his upper lip, his mouth looked like a gaping hole filled with sharp yellow teeth.

But it was his eyes that struck most terror in Jessica's heart. They were pale blue, the color of ice, and they glistened with madness. "The forest will be grateful," he whispered.

I'm going to die, she thought.

With Tanya slumped over his shoulder, the man headed deeper into the forest, dragging Jessica along by the hair. Her whole body throbbed with pain. She tried to ignore it, to focus on memorizing the path they were taking. But the trees all looked alike; each boulder seemed to be an exact copy of the last.

Tanya's limp arms swayed against the man's back with every step he took. The purple friendship bracelet Jessica had made for her was still fastened on her tiny wrist.

Hot, angry tears streamed down Jessica's face. A thought flashed across her mind: *Tanya is going to die, too.* But a voice inside Jessica's head screamed, *No!*

Acting on blind instinct, she reached for Tanya's wrist.

Chapter 11

That's it! Elizabeth thought, her face hot with anger. Fuming, she marched over to Nicole. "I've had just about enough of your silly little games."

Nicole flashed her a sickeningly sweet smile. "Don't be such a bad sport, Elizabeth. You know the rules of the game—I caught Joey, and now he's my prisoner. Sorry if that makes you jealous."

"Oh, grow up!" Elizabeth said. "I'm sick and tired of your immature behavior. You're nothing but a spoiled, nasty little brat. I know you're Maria's friend, but that doesn't excuse all the mean pranks you've pulled. I'm telling you right here and now—I'm not putting up with you anymore."

Nicole gaped at her with a look of exaggerated innocence. "Me? Mean pranks? I don't know

131

what you're talking about, Dizzy Lizzie."

Elizabeth bristled. "Come off it, Nicole. You know exactly what I'm talking about."

Nicole shook her head, chuckling. "I assure you, I really don't know what you mean."

"I mean your wood-chopping act in the forest after dinner this evening," Elizabeth said. "I suppose you don't know anything about that."

Nicole frowned as if she were genuinely confused, and looked directly into Elizabeth's eyes. "I honestly don't know what you're talking about."

What a great actress! Elizabeth thought hotly.

Joey stepped forward. "Quit lying, Nicole. Last week Elizabeth and I both heard you chopping wood, and then I saw you running away."

Elizabeth gave him a warm look, thankful for his support. Nicole's face turned bright red. She lowered her eyes and kicked at the ground. "OK, fine. I'll admit I did try to scare her a few times. But not today."

"I don't believe you," Elizabeth said.

Nicole's nostrils flared. "I don't care if you believe me or not. I've been busy with my team all day, and that's the truth."

"Someone's coming, you guys," Winston called. Elizabeth had forgotten all about him and was surprised to see that he'd climbed to the top of a huge boulder.

A few seconds later, Maria came along, gingerly leading her prisoner, Tad, who was one of the ten-year-olds in Winston's group. "I've got another one, Nicole," Maria gloated.

No one spoke. Maria's smile disappeared. "What's going on?" she asked. She turned to Nicole. "What have you been up to now?"

Nicole stood with her fists pressed into her sides. "Why do you always assume everything's my fault?" she demanded.

Maria shrugged. "Because usually it is."

Tad applauded enthusiastically. "All right! Is there going to be a girl fight?"

"Come on, Tad," Joey said, discreetly leading the boy away. "Let's get out of here."

"I'm coming with you," Winston said, sliding down the rock.

When the guys had left, Nicole turned to Maria. "It's not my fault this time. Elizabeth and Joey accused me of trying to scare Elizabeth in the woods today. I didn't do it, but of course they don't believe me."

"It's true," Maria told Elizabeth. "Nicole has been running around all day, keeping tabs on all the events. She hasn't taken a single break."

Nicole stuck her tongue out at Elizabeth. "So there, Miss Know-it-all!"

Maria rolled her eyes and sighed. "I wish you two would get a grip."

Nicole sneered at Elizabeth and said, "Give it up, Maria. It's never going to happen."

Elizabeth nodded absently, her mind beginning to spin in a new direction. *Joey and I both heard that ax this afternoon. If it wasn't Nicole, then who was it?*

Elizabeth's gaze shifted to the dark woods surrounding the path. Her chest felt tight, making it difficult to breathe. More than ever, Elizabeth was positive that something sinister was going on, something far more dangerous than her rivalry with Nicole.

By the time Elizabeth returned to the main field, capture the flag had turned into a screaming frenzy. Jennifer and Ashley ran up to her, their eyes glittering with excitement.

"It's the ax man's ghost!" Jennifer cried.

Ashley nodded. Her wavy blond hair was a wild, tangled mess around her face. "Crazy Freddy is back."

"What happened?" Elizabeth forced her voice to remain calm and even.

"He's come to kill us," Ashley screeched.

Jennifer clutched Elizabeth's arm with her sticky hand. "You have to save us, Diz—I mean Liz."

Maria and Nicole arrived after Elizabeth. Nicole looked furious. Marching ahead, she barked out commands like a military leader, calling the red team to order in a voice that meant business.

"What's all this about?" Maria asked Elizabeth.

Ashley and Jennifer answered in unison, "Crazy Freddy is back!"

"Some of the kids heard him in the woods," Ashley added.

A few yards away, two of the senior counselors, Rose and Suzanne, were frantically trying to gather the younger campers into a circle. "What's this about Crazy Freddy?" Elizabeth asked them.

Suzanne appeared to be at the end of her patience. "I wish I knew. First we heard a groaning noise coming from the woods on this side of the field, and then there was a loud clanging noise coming from the other side." Her lips stretched into a tight smile. "Now, thanks to someone's twisted sense of humor, we have mass hysteria on our hands."

"This is terrible," Elizabeth said. A creepy feeling crawled up her spine.

Rose smiled reassuringly. "Hey, don't worry, Elizabeth. It's just a practical joke. We get pranks like this every year. I've even pulled a few myself," she added.

Elizabeth nodded, wanting to believe Rose's

135

simple explanation. *If only I knew where Jessica was*, she thought. *Then I wouldn't be nearly as worried.*

"Hey, Elizabeth," Nicole called, walking toward her, waving a white tissue. "Don't get any ideas, wonder twin. This isn't surrender. Let's take a break to get our teams under control. Everyone is going crazy."

"I agree," Elizabeth said.

"How about that!" Nicole said, her voice dripping with sarcasm. "The wonder twin agrees with me. Guess you're not as dumb as I figured."

Elizabeth ignored the barb and put her energy into being a team captain. It took a while, but she finally managed to gather her players in a huddle behind the main lodge. "We can't let this silly trick get in the way of winning," she told them. "Time's running out, and we need the points. We've captured seven of their players and—"

"Where's Tanya?" Sarah blurted out suddenly. Her dark eyes were filled with a look of alarm.

Elizabeth swallowed her irritation. *Sarah is only seven*, she reminded herself. "I don't know where Tanya is," she said evenly. "Maybe she went to the bathroom. Now, as I was saying—"

"But she wouldn't go all by herself," Sarah insisted.

Tiffany flipped back her blond hair and fluttered her long eyelashes. "Maybe Crazy Freddy ate her."

Elizabeth glared at the conceited thirteen-year-old. "We don't need any of that, Tiffany."

Sarah started to cry.

Elizabeth closed her eyes and began counting to ten in her head. *One, two, three . . .*

Odette and Samantha, the twins from Georgia, volunteered to go look for Tanya. Sarah wiped her face and scrambled off behind them.

The blue team continued talking over game tactics. A few minutes later, the girls returned. Sarah was sobbing. "We checked everywhere," Odette said urgently. "The bathrooms, the cabins, the boathouse . . ."

"We even looked in the boys' bathrooms," Samantha added with a giggle.

Aaron Dallas groaned. "Just what we need. Teenyboppers in the guys' john! What kind of a place is this?"

Buford, a member of the red team, popped out from behind the building. "It's the enemy!" Bryan shouted.

A chorus of jeers rose from the blue team. Buford pushed his thick glasses high up on his nose and raised his hands in the air. "I come unarmed. I've been sent to tell you that the time-out is over."

"Hey, Buford," Aaron said, "better be careful. I just found out the girls are sending spies into the boys' bathroom."

Samantha shoved Aaron. "It was an emergency," she said in an exaggerated southern drawl.

Elizabeth turned to Buford. "Tell Nicole we need more time. Tanya Mathis is missing."

A few minutes after Buford had left, Nicole herself sauntered over. She stood with her hands on her hips, poised for battle. "What's going on, Elizabeth? This had better not be a trick."

Elizabeth glared back at her. "That's your style, Nicole. Not mine."

Sarah and Stephanie came up behind Elizabeth. "We can't find Tanya. She's gone, Nicole."

"Is that true?" Nicole asked.

Elizabeth nodded gravely. "We've already checked all the obvious places."

"OK. I guess the game will have to wait," Nicole said, eyeing Elizabeth with a measuring look. "I'll go get Lacey."

Rose, Suzanne, Derek, Joey, and the other senior counselors gathered everyone together in the main field to organize a search. The players from the prisons were brought in to help. Lacey banged on her pot, calling the group to attention, and laid down the ground rules. No one was to go alone or to wander off camp property. Then everyone broke up into small groups to look for Tanya.

Elizabeth and Maria searched the woods that bordered the main field. "I'm worried about Jessica," Elizabeth said, pointing her flashlight into the darkness. "I have this strange feeling that she's in trouble."

Maria snorted. "One missing girl at a time, OK? If I know Jessica, she's probably having a great time at this very moment—and she's certainly not worrying about you."

"I know," Elizabeth said. "I keep telling myself the same thing." She shone her light over a tall boulder and around the base of a tree.

"What's that on the ground?" Maria said.

"Where?" Elizabeth followed the beam of Maria's flashlight. Something that looked like a piece of brightly colored string lay half buried in a clump of springy moss.

Elizabeth picked it up and recognized it immediately. "It's the friendship bracelet Jessica made for Tanya. It looks as if the clasp was pulled apart."

"Come on, let's go get the others," Maria said.

When they returned to the main area of the camp, Maria ran to find Lacey while Elizabeth talked to the kids on the field. Joey stood by her side as she held up Tanya's bracelet and explained where she and Maria had found it.

The five remaining Wanna-bes were devastated. "Something terrible must have happened! Tanya said she wouldn't ever take it off for the rest of her life!" Maggie cried.

Elizabeth turned to Nicole and Joey. Without another word, the three of them sprang into action, calling everyone in from the woods. Suzanne, Rose, and Derek gathered the campers together in the field.

Lacey banged on her pot. "I know everyone is upset about Tanya, but we must stay calm. It's getting dark. We can't have everyone running around in the woods. I'm going to call the state police for help."

"I think we should search the area where Elizabeth and Maria found Tanya's bracelet," Nicole protested.

"I agree," Elizabeth said, amazed that she was taking Nicole's side. "Tanya might have fallen and sprained her ankle or something."

Lacey glared at them. "No arguments! I'll be back as soon as I've called the police."

As Lacey turned to go, Joey came over and stood next to Elizabeth. "I wonder . . ." He spoke softly, as if he were talking to himself. "There's an abandoned cabin . . ." Suddenly he squeezed Elizabeth's hand and said, "I'll be right back. I have an idea where Tanya might be."

"No, Joey!" Elizabeth called frantically as she watched him run toward the woods. "It's too dangerous to go out there alone."

At the same time Nicole yelled, "Joey, don't!"

"I'll be fine," he called over his shoulder. Elizabeth and Nicole stood motionless, side by side, and watched as he disappeared into the darkness of the woods.

Jessica fell with a loud thud onto the hardwood floor of an old, rundown cabin. As she tried to take a breath, a man's leather boot kicked her in the side, knocking the wind out of her again. "Get out of the way," he growled.

Her muscles screamed with pain as she raised herself to her hands and knees and crawled to a corner. She backed up against the wall and huddled there in a fetal position.

The man lifted Tanya's body from his shoulder and dropped her on the floor. Jessica's heart lurched in anguish. For one terrifying moment she thought Tanya was dead. Then she saw the rise and fall of Tanya's chest and sighed with relief. But Tanya's face, arms, and legs were covered with dirty gashes and bruises. The lace edging on the sleeve of her blue T-shirt was stained with blood. Jessica's eyes filled with hot, angry tears.

"Oh, quit your bellyaching," the man's voice

ordered. "The forest doesn't want a crybaby, and neither do I." He stomped to the door. "I'll be right back, blondie. Don't go away."

As soon as he was gone Jessica scooped Tanya up in her arms. The man had left the door open, and she could hear him chopping wood outside the cabin. The sound filled her with terror.

"We have to get out of here," she whispered close to Tanya's ear, even though she knew the child was beyond reach. "There has to be a way."

She studied her surroundings, searching for a clue. The cabin was small and dark, with shadows flickering across the walls like dancing demons. The only light came from a smoky oil lamp on a decrepit wooden table in the center of the room. A three-legged stool and a wooden crate were the only other pieces of furniture.

She forced herself to think of an escape plan. There was only one door, plus two small windows. *Maybe I could hit him in the head with the stool, grab Tanya, and rush past him to the door—*

The man's heavy footsteps creaked on the front step. "Honey, I'm home," he said in a creepy-sounding falsetto.

Jessica looked up and gasped. He was standing in the doorway, holding the ax at his side and a coil of rope looped over his shoulder.

He staggered to the corner and leaned over

Jessica. His pale eyes glimmered as he reached out and touched her hair, pushing it behind her ears. "So very lovely," he whispered, running a long, yellowed fingernail along the side of her neck.

Jessica froze in terror, all of her senses alert. She could smell the stench of old smoke and sweat on his shirt, the damp, stale odor of his breath.

Suddenly he tipped his head back and laughed, the serrated line of his teeth flashing like a knife in his patchy dark beard. He set the ax down on the floor behind him and uncoiled the rope. Jessica cowered deeper into the corner and wrapped her arms more tightly around Tanya, as much for her own comfort as to protect the child.

"This is where it gets interesting, blondie," he said. "I've been waiting a long time for you, and so has the forest."

Jessica glanced behind him at the stool, then at the door, mentally gauging the distance. *Could I make it?* she wondered.

As if he'd read her thoughts, the man grabbed her elbow with the force of an iron clamp until she screamed in pain. "Let's get one thing straight, blondie. Unless you want me to chop off your little friend's head right here and now, you'd better not try anything sneaky." He looked at Tanya and chuckled. "Although that could be fun, too."

Trembling, Jessica shook her head. "I p-promise . . . I won't," she stammered.

"That's better." He tied Jessica and Tanya together, binding their legs and arms so that they could hardly move.

When he was finished, he sat back and grinned, as if he were admiring his handiwork.

The ax was at his side. In the flickering yellow light of the oil lamp, the blade gleamed. *Please find me, Elizabeth!* Jessica screamed in her mind, sending a desperate signal to her twin. *Before it's too late.*

Chapter 12

"Can you imagine the trouble we'd be in if Lacey found me in here?" Bo asked with a laugh as he helped himself to another shrimp. "She'd probably break out in hives."

Lila giggled. "It serves her right for making up all those stupid rules." She and Bo were snuggled together in the girls' cabin, sharing a late supper of cold shrimp and tropical fruit that had been delivered that afternoon by the ever-faithful Western Meadowlark air cargo service.

Lila had wanted to create something as wonderful for Bo as he had for her with Paris in springtime. She'd decided to give him a day on Bali Ha'i, his dream island. With fresh flowers and a few items she'd ordered from the Home Splendor catalog, she had redecorated the cabin in a Polynesian theme. She'd hung yards of colorful fabric over the dingy walls and set candles, baskets of flowers, and potted palms everywhere.

"I wonder how our teams are doing out there," Lila said, reaching for a slice of pineapple. "Remember, if the red team wins, you have to send me roses every week for the next year." It didn't bother her in the least that she and Bo were shirking their duties in the color war. The idea of jumping around in potato sacks or playing catch with raw eggs didn't appeal to people with their refined tastes.

"You're on, Lila. And if my team wins, I get a new picture of you every week to hang on my wall. I want your face to be the first thing I see in the morning and the last thing at night." Bo reached over and touched her hand. "You're the most beautiful girl I've ever seen."

Lila beamed with happiness as she gazed into his dark eyes. By candlelight—any light—he was clearly the hottest guy she'd ever met. Usually a girl had to choose between brains, class, and looks in a boyfriend, but Bo had it all. "I hate to see this day end," she said wistfully.

Bo brought her hand to his lips and kissed it gently. "Don't worry, Lila. This is only the beginning."

*　　*　　*

A crowd was gathered around a huge bonfire when Lila and Bo arrived at the main field. Lila looked around for Jessica, eager to compare notes with her on their romantic adventures. She was sure her date with Bo would easily outclass Jessica's date with Paul.

Maria came running from the direction of the activities buildings. "Lacey's still talking to the police," she announced.

"What's going on?" Lila asked. "Who won the color war?"

Suzanne turned to her, frowning. "We never got to finish the game. Where have *you* been all day?"

"Bali Ha'i," Lila answered flippantly. She and Bo walked over to where the Sulky Six were huddled together near the fire. "Why is Lacey talking to the police?" Lila asked.

"Because someone was making strange noises in the woods," Odette answered. "And now we can't find Tanya Mathis."

Lila told Bo she'd be right back and went over to Elizabeth. "Where is Jessica?" she whispered.

Elizabeth pulled her aside. "She's not back from her date with Paul. It's after ten o'clock, and I'm worried sick about her," she said anxiously.

"Don't be. Punctuality isn't exactly one of Jessica's strong points," Lila reminded her. "She'll come back when she's good and ready—even if she has to steal a horse to do it."

Elizabeth nodded. "I know. I just wish she'd hurry up and get here."

Nicole ran up to them. "Elizabeth, we can't just sit around. Joey should never have gone out there by himself."

Lila blinked, completely confused. *Nicole and Elizabeth are discussing Joey without trying to scratch each other's eyes out?* she marveled. "Will someone tell me what's going on?" she demanded.

Elizabeth sighed wearily. "Tanya disappeared. We found her friendship bracelet in the woods, and Joey went off to find her by himself."

"To prove what a macho man he is!" Nicole snapped.

"Anyway, you're right," Elizabeth told Nicole. "Waiting around here isn't helping anything. Let's split up into pairs and search for them. But no one goes alone," she added.

Lila returned to Bo's side and wrapped her arm around his waist. *Thank goodness he's not like Joey and doesn't have to prove what a man he is by taking stupid risks,* she thought.

Nicole and Elizabeth began to call for volunteers to search for Tanya and Joey.

"Hold it!" Suzanne hollered at them. "You girls

heard what Lacey said. Everyone stays put until she comes back."

Nicole puffed out her chest and looked Suzanne in the eye. "Try to stop us," she dared.

I have to admit, the girl has spunk, Lila thought as she rested her head on Bo's shoulder and watched the drama unfold.

"Lila," Bo whispered in her ear, "I'm going to join the search."

Lila jerked her head up and glared at him. "You can't be serious! There are animals out there, Bo. Not to mention possibly ghosts and a legendary ax murderer."

He traced the line of her eyebrows with his finger. "I have to."

"No, you don't," she replied. "I was just thinking how wonderful it was that you didn't have to risk your neck just to prove that you're a macho man."

"This is different," he countered. "I'd be risking my neck to look for a kid who's lost in the woods. Believe me, I know how scared she must be feeling right now."

"Oh, Bo." Lila hugged him tightly, her heart brimming with love and admiration. "OK," she said, "but I'm going with you."

Elizabeth looked across the stream, trying to estimate the width of the churning water. It had to be at least five feet, but there wasn't any other place to cross. The spot was right between two waterfalls, with a solid rock wall to the left and a sharp cliff to the right. The roar of crashing water underscored the danger.

From the opposite side of the stream, Nicole waved her flashlight. "Come on, Wakefield, jump! You can come back and enjoy the view some other time."

Elizabeth glared at her. "Will you be quiet? I'm trying to concentrate." There was a flat, slippery-looking rock in the center to use as a stepping stone. But if she lost her footing, she'd be swept over the waterfall to certain death.

"We don't have all day, wonder twin." Nicole reached out her hand. "Just do it."

Elizabeth drew in a deep breath and nodded. Gathering her courage, she took a few steps back for a running start and jumped.

She missed the flat stone, and her hiking boot touched down in the icy water with a huge splash. Then, gripping Nicole's hand to steady herself, Elizabeth leaped forward to safety—and slammed right into Nicole.

Both of them toppled over in a heap. "My hat!" Nicole screeched. "It fell off."

Elizabeth pulled herself up and grabbed her flashlight. She aimed the beam at the stream just in time to see the red baseball cap rushing over the cascade. "There it goes," Elizabeth said dryly.

Nicole punched her shoulder. "You did that on purpose, Dizzy Lizzie. Admit it!"

Elizabeth gave her a condescending look. "No, I didn't. Unlike you, Nicole, I don't play childish games."

Nicole stood up and grumbled, "Picnic's over, wonder twin. We have a little kid and an idiot guy to rescue. At this rate, they'll die of exposure before we find them."

Instantly sober, Elizabeth followed. The steep hill gave way to a level stretch of pine forest. Their footsteps made scratching noises on the bed of dry needles. Every few minutes they stopped and called out Tanya's name.

Although Elizabeth didn't like spending any more time with Nicole than she had to, when the JCs had split up to cover the area around the camp, it had seemed natural for the two of them to be paired up to search. After being bound together by mutual dislike, fierce competition, and their attraction to Joey, it seemed they would be bound to each other until the crisis came to an end. Besides, Elizabeth wanted to be there if Nicole found Joey first.

Watching the rigid set of her shoulders as they traipsed through the woods, Elizabeth reluctantly admitted to herself that Nicole did have a few positive traits. She was physically strong and agile, and she had a great sense of direction. Elizabeth also realized that Nicole was as desperate as she was to find Tanya, and just as worried about Joey.

Suddenly a tall figure dropped from a tree. Elizabeth jumped back, and Nicole grabbed him from behind. He shrugged himself free, then covered his eyes as Elizabeth shone the light on his face. "Paul?" Elizabeth gulped with relief and lowered the flashlight.

"What's going on?" he demanded.

"Oh, Paul, thank goodness you're here," Elizabeth said. "Tanya disappeared from camp, and we found her friendship bracelet in the woods."

He looked at her and Nicole with a strange expression. "Where's Jessica?"

Elizabeth felt a cold, prickly sensation crawl over her skin. "She was with you, wasn't she?"

"She was," Paul said. "But we split up, and she sneaked into camp."

"I just knew it!" Elizabeth shrieked. "Crazy Freddy has both of them."

Nicole snorted. "Get real, Diz. Even you can't be dumb enough to believe that story."

Elizabeth didn't know what to believe anymore. But what she did know for sure was that her twin radar was setting off screaming alarms in her mind that blared *Jessica is in trouble!* She began to shake, sobbing hysterically.

"Oh, *please*," Nicole groaned. "You can't fall apart now, wonder twin."

Elizabeth struggled for control, but her body refused to obey. She felt as if she were being attacked by massive bolts of electricity.

"This is just great!" Nicole muttered. She took Elizabeth's hand and tugged her into motion. "Come along, Dizzy Lizzie. We're taking you back to camp."

"I'll keep looking around here," Paul said.

Elizabeth stopped and turned to him. Even in the darkness, she could see how worried he was. "Please let us know as soon as you find something," she pleaded.

With her hands tied behind her back, Jessica struggled until her shoulders ached, but the rope around her wrists remained tight, digging into her flesh.

Curled up in her lap, Tanya stirred. Her little arms and legs were bound at the wrists and ankles, and a rope around her neck connected her to Jessica. Tanya's lip was cut and swollen, and a smear of dried blood stained her chin.

Jessica wondered how anyone could hurt a

small, defenseless child. *Only a monster could,* her mind answered. She looked over at their kidnapper as he sat on the wooden crate, sharpening his ax with a whetstone, the high-pitched grinding sound setting her teeth on edge. His pale blue eyes seemed to radiate with an unnatural light. *Monster?* Yes, the description fit.

Tanya began to whimper softly. Afraid of drawing the monster's attention, Jessica lowered her lips to Tanya's ear and whispered, "Hush, sweetie. It's OK."

"My head hurts." Tanya's voice was thin and scratchy.

Jessica swallowed, tears filling her eyes. "Everything is going to be all right," she said, forcing her voice to come out evenly, as if she weren't afraid for their lives.

Tanya's chin quivered. "I wanna go home."

"I know you do." Jessica closed her eyes. The hopelessness of their situation felt like a ton of bricks on her chest. But she couldn't stand by and watch Tanya suffer. She had to try something, anything.

Bracing her nerves, Jessica cleared her throat. "Excuse me, um, Mr. Freddy?"

He looked over at her, his forehead creased in a deep frown. "Mr. Freddy? What kind of a stupid name is that? I'm Cobra, darlin', Frank Cobra." He licked the tip of his finger and ran it along the sharpened edge of the ax blade. "I don't usually tell people my name," he said in a casual tone of voice. "But where you girls are going, you won't be able to tell anyone, and the forest already knows my name."

Jessica closed her eyes. *He's insane*, she thought hopelessly.

All of a sudden a furious pounding sounded at the door. With a combination of hope and dread, Jessica's heart banged against her ribs.

The sound of Joey's voice called to her. "Jessica, are you in there? Open up!"

The monster muttered a curse and lunged forward, still holding the ax. Jessica gasped as he crouched down in front of her and Tanya and pressed his thick, grimy hands over their mouths. "Seems I've struck pay dirt," he whispered against Jessica's ear. The brush of his lips made her skin crawl. "The more the merrier, right, blondie?"

He lifted the ax, and Jessica's whole body stiffened in anticipation of a deadly blow. In her arms, Tanya trembled.

As if reading Jessica's fear, he chuckled softly. "Not until the full moon sets, darlin'. Sacrifice is for sunrise." He used the ax blade to cut the ropes that bound the two girls, then yanked Jessica to her feet.

The pounding on the door continued. "Jessica, can you hear me?" Joey yelled.

Run away, Joey! Jessica screamed in her mind. *He's going to kill us all!*

Cobra glanced at the door. "Let Mr. Hotshot in, blondie."

"I won't do it," she said.

He grabbed a fistful of her hair and jerked her head back, forcing her to look directly into his face. Jessica recoiled in horror from the demonic look in his pale blue eyes. "I think you will," he hissed.

He shoved Jessica toward the door, then grabbed Tanya by the hair. Holding the ax blade against Tanya's throat, he stood behind the door and winked at Jessica. "Be a good girl, blondie. Answer the door, nice and easy."

Tanya's face was ghostly white, her purple bruises standing out in stark relief. Her eyes were focused straight ahead, as if she'd gone into shock.

Jessica swallowed hard and walked to the door. Opening it a crack, she tried to signal for Joey to run away, without alerting the monster. But Joey pushed the door open and brazenly rushed into the cabin—and into the trap.

Cobra stepped up behind him and slammed the ax handle down on his head with a loud crack. Joey slumped to the floor, out cold.

Jessica pulled Tanya into her arms and held her tightly, both of them sobbing. Cobra planted his booted foot on Joey's chest and turned to them with a self-satisfied smile. "The forest will be very pleased come sunrise."

Chapter 13

Huddled near the bonfire, Elizabeth looked up and saw Paul walking toward her with a grim look on his face. He was alone. "You didn't see any sign of them?" she asked as he sat down beside her.

He shook his head. "I'm sorry."

Elizabeth shivered. The flames did little to ward off the icy chill in her bones. Something was wrong; she knew it with gut certainty.

Lacey's voice suddenly boomed forth from the loudspeaker, startling Elizabeth. "All campers and counselors, return to the bonfire. I repeat, everyone at Camp Echo Mountain is to report to the bonfire immediately."

A surge of terror squeezed Elizabeth's throat. "I wonder what's going on," she said. Paul looked equally scared.

Lacey came running out to the field. "I'm in deep trouble now," Paul whispered to Elizabeth.

But Lacey seemed too upset to notice him. She sent the campers to the main lodge, then turned to address the counselors. Her usual in-charge-and-under-control expression was gone. In its place was a look of pure, open panic—scaring Elizabeth even more.

"I have some terrible news," Lacey announced. "I've just learned that a wanted man was last sighted in North Dakota at a resort camp near Cedar Canyon, which isn't far from the Montana border. Someone there was murdered and—"

She paused, raising her hand to her throat. Her fingers were shaking. "The police will be here soon. In the meantime, let's get everyone settled in at the lodge. No one is to go back to their cabins for any reason whatsoever."

"We can't wait for the police," Elizabeth said. "We have to do something right now."

Lacey shook her head frantically. "No arguments, please! I'm going to need each and every one of you to help keep the campers calm. The worst thing we could possibly do is to get in the way of the police."

Just then Nicole and Maria came running out of the woods, both of them out of breath. "Joey is missing, too," Nicole called urgently.

Aaron looked around and frowned. "Lila and

Bo haven't come back, either. It's strange for Bo to stay in the woods for over an hour." A few of the guys snickered.

Lacey clapped her hands frantically. "Everyone in the lodge, now! Before more of us disappear."

Nicole turned to Elizabeth. A meaningful look passed between them. "We can't wait," Nicole whispered.

Elizabeth nodded. "I know. We have to find them now." A frightened voice in her mind added, *If it's not already too late.* "I'll lose my mind if I sit around waiting for the police," Paul muttered. He, Elizabeth, and Nicole hung back as the others headed to the lodge.

Elizabeth nervously gazed at the dark expanse of woods beyond the field. "Joey mentioned something about an abandoned cabin. Do either of you know where it is?"

"I wonder if it's the same cabin my friends and I used to use as our clubhouse when we were little," Paul said. "It's only two or three miles from here."

"That's the best lead we have so far," Nicole said. "Let's go."

Bo traced an invisible line in the night sky with his finger. "By keeping our direction oriented to Polaris, we know we haven't been walking around in circles. Although I have no idea where we are," he added in a dejected tone.

"I'm very impressed that you know the names of all the stars," Lila said, rotating her head from side to side to ease the stiffness in her neck. She'd been craning her neck to look up as Bo pointed out the various constellations and planets in the sky. She and Bo were sitting side by side on a huge rock, where they had stopped to rest after having hiked for hours.

Lila rested her head on Bo's shoulder. "I wish one of those stars pointed out the direction of the nearest restaurant—one that takes plastic, though, since neither of us brought any cash," she said wistfully. "Shoot," she added with a weary laugh, "give me a hotdog stand and I'll hock my gold bracelet. I'm starving, Bo."

He put his arm around her shoulders. "Me too."

She kissed the side of his neck. His skin felt warm and enticing against her lips. "I guess if I have to be lost in the woods with someone, I'm glad it's you."

Bo chuckled and pulled her close for a heart-stopping kiss, sending hot thrills up and down her spine.

"Very glad," she murmured, running her fingers through his lush, curly brown hair. "By the way, how do you know so much about astronomy? We've already established the fact that you're not the outdoorsy type."

"I'm just interested, that's all," he said. "But if you're getting bored, I'll stop talking about it. I guess I've been rambling on to keep my mind off . . . um . . ." He began to breathe rapidly.

Pressed close to his side, Lila felt his heart pounding. *He's terrified*, she thought. "It's OK, Bo," she said, stroking his back. "We're here together, and that's all that matters."

"I feel like such a wimp," he groaned.

She leaned back and looked him in the eye. "Well, you're not. Doing the right thing even though you're scared to death—that's the true measure of courage. As far as I'm concerned, Beauregard Creighton the third, you're the bravest hero in the world."

"You mean that?" he asked, sounding hopeful.

She kissed him soundly. "Of course I do. And if you want to talk all night about stars, planets, or anything else, you go right ahead."

"Thanks." He cupped her face in his hands and gazed at her with a look of wonder, as if she were a priceless treasure. "Lila, I love you."

"I love you, too," she whispered.

"Want to hear about my new telescope?" he asked. "It can pick up Jupiter's spot."

Lila giggled and snuggled tightly against him. If anyone had ever told her that she'd someday enjoy listening to an astronomy lecture, she would have laughed. But somehow everything Bo said was fascinating. "I'd love to," she replied.

"It's just up ahead," Paul whispered to Nicole and Elizabeth. Peering through the spaces between the trees, Nicole could barely make out the outline of a small cabin in the moonlight. A sharp pang of fear rose inside her, but she pushed it back down. "I think we should turn off our flashlights," she said, proud that her voice sounded calm. She wasn't about to lose her dignity, the way Dizzy Lizzie had earlier.

They stood in the shadowy darkness awhile, all eyes watching the cabin. Finally Paul said, "I'm going in."

Nicole clasped his arm, holding him back. "Wait a minute. We can't just go prancing up to the front door like we're paying a little neighborly visit. We don't know who—or what—is in there."

Paul shook his arm free. "You're right. You and Elizabeth stay here. I'll go alone."

Nicole grabbed his arm again. "Just what we need, another idiot macho man!" she exclaimed hotly.

"Jessica and my sister might be in there!" he exclaimed.

163

Nicole turned to Elizabeth for support, but the wonder twin was glassy-eyed and shaking like a wet cat. Exasperated, Nicole threw up her hands. "Will you get real?" she said to Paul. "I understand how every guy wants to be a big hero, but come on—we don't even know if our people are in there. Do you really want to be featured in the next police bulletin as the victim of some crazy murderer?"

Elizabeth looked at her with a faraway expression. "Jessica is inside that cabin. I can *feel* her."

Nicole snorted. "Thank you, Miss New Age California. OK, let's assume they're all in the cabin, including our deranged camp killer. We still can't go sashaying over there. We need a plan, folks."

"What do you have in mind?" Paul asked.

Nicole thought for a moment. "I wonder if there's another way to get inside. . . . Paul, why don't you creep around behind the cabin and check it out? Then if you see that our friends are in there with some knife-wielding maniac, Elizabeth and I will cover for you while you sneak inside and rescue them."

"And how will you cover me?" he asked.

"We'll act as decoys and draw the bad guy out the front door." She saw the hesitation in his eyes. "It'll work," she insisted. "Do you have a better idea?"

He shook his head. "No, but I wish I did. OK, let's try it. Wait for my signal."

Nicole watched him disappear in the shadows around the cabin. Next to her, Elizabeth stood motionless, like a marble statue. Her fair complexion seemed to glow in the moonlight, giving her the dreamy look of a princess in distress.

A spark of envy flickered in Nicole's gut. "You know, Diz," she began, unable to resist baiting the wonder twin, "even if your sister is in there, she might already be dead."

Something flickered in the depths of Elizabeth's blue-green eyes. "No," she said calmly. "Jessica is alive. But she's in grave danger."

Nicole rolled her eyes. "Oh, please! Did you read her aura through the cabin walls, or was it your spirit guide who told you?"

"I just know, that's all," Elizabeth replied.

Paul's signal came at that moment, a low whistle from the other side of the clearing. Nicole took a deep breath and nudged Elizabeth. "There's our cue, Wakefield."

The girls stepped out of the shadows, calling out Jessica's and Tanya's names. As they got nearer to the cabin, Nicole noticed a small window on the side wall. She gestured to Elizabeth, then crept over to take a peek.

Standing on tiptoe, Nicole wiped a circle in the thick layer of grime that coated the glass pane and peered through the window. Her heart jumped to her throat. Jessica and Tanya were huddled on the floor, tied up together. *And Joey!* Nicole gasped, pressing her fist against her mouth. Joey was lying on the floor, very still. Too still. He seemed to be unconscious. *Or dead!* her mind screamed.

Nicole moved away from the window, her body throbbing with red-hot fury. *Whoever did this is going to pay!* she thought.

As she was about to step out from behind the corner of the cabin, the front door swung open with a loud crash. Nicole flattened herself against the wall and held her breath.

Heavy footsteps pounded across the porch. Suddenly Elizabeth screamed. Nicole leaned sideways and looked just in time to see the dark, shadowy figure of a man grab Elizabeth by her long ponytail. Then, with heart-clutching dread, Nicole noticed the ax in his hand.

Still screaming, Elizabeth struggled to get free. The man raised the ax and held the blade against Elizabeth's long, white neck. Nicole squeezed her eyes shut and pressed her hand against her mouth, holding back her own urge to scream.

"Well, lookee here," the shadow growled. "Another blondie, as beautiful as the first."

Nicole opened her eyes and saw the man yank Elizabeth's hair. With peals of cruel laugher, he jerked her backward toward the door of the cabin.

Elizabeth howled in pain, still struggling valiantly against him.

Nicole sniffed, vaguely aware of the tears streaming down her face. Even with all the animosity between them, she couldn't bear the idea of losing Elizabeth this way. The wonder twin had stood up to every challenge Nicole had thrown at her—and had returned a few hard kicks of her own. Elizabeth was the only other girl at camp who'd been willing to break the rules and risk everything to save Jessica, Tanya, and Joey. Even now, in the clutches of an armed madman, Elizabeth was still fighting valiantly. *She's the first worthwhile rival I've ever had,* Nicole thought.

So do something! her mind shouted. Her whole body felt numb, as if her nerves had completely shut down. Suddenly an idea began to take shape. Nicole breathed deeply and plunged forward.

"Oh, yes, please kill Elizabeth!" she yelled. Clapping her hands at arm's length in front of her, she marched into the clearing and ad-libbed the best dramatic lines she'd ever created. "Bravo for you, my good man. Off with her head! Kill her! She's nothing but trouble."

It worked. Momentarily distracted, the man jerked his head toward Nicole and lowered his arm long enough for Elizabeth to twist away from him. But as Nicole turned to run, she felt his hand land heavily on her shoulder. Then his arm looped around her neck.

Elizabeth hesitated, her eyes clouded with indecision.

"Go, Elizabeth!" Nicole shouted. "Save the others!"

Chapter 14

Jessica heard the commotion outside the cabin, and her muscles tensed, ready to spring to action. "Listen to me, Tanya," she said softly. "You stick close by me, no matter what happens, OK?"

Tanya nodded solemnly, her wide, watery eyes fixed on Jessica's face in a look of complete trust. Jessica gulped. *We're going to make it*, she vowed.

She nudged Joey with her knee. "Wake up," she whispered urgently. "Elizabeth and Nicole are here, and maybe some of the others."

Suddenly a rock came crashing through the back window. Jessica leaned forward to protect Tanya's head as a spray of shattered glass fell across the floor. When she looked up, her jaw dropped. Paul was climbing through the window, his muscular leg hooked over the windowsill.

Jessica felt as if her heart were ready to explode. She couldn't remember ever being so happy to see someone.

He ran to her and deftly cut everyone loose with his pocketknife. "Elizabeth and Nicole are outside," he whispered as he helped Jessica to her feet. He looked into her eyes and asked, "Are you OK?"

Jessica gave him a tremulous smile. "Now I am."

He kissed her quickly, then touched Tanya's hair. His hand shook slightly. "We have to get out of here," he said.

Jessica scooped Tanya up in her arms, ignoring the painful stiffness in her shoulders. Joey was still helplessly groggy. Paul helped him stand and supported his weight as the four of them rushed to the door.

"Hurry, Elizabeth! The others are inside," Nicole shouted.

Elizabeth's legs refused to move. Paralyzed with fear, she watched helplessly as the man raised his ax to Nicole's throat. "No!" Elizabeth screamed.

Suddenly Joey staggered out of the cabin with his arm draped around Paul's neck. In the shimmering moonlight, Joey's face looked as white as a ghost's, as if he were in terrible pain. Elizabeth's throat squeezed tightly. *He's been hurt!* she thought, trembling. *And now Nicole . . .*

Joey stumbled on the porch steps. Before Paul could catch him, Joey pitched forward and crashed into the madman, knocking the ax out of his hand. Then Jessica ran out of the cabin with Tanya.

Elizabeth blinked. Everything seemed to be happening too fast to be real. Joey, Paul, Nicole, and the man fell to the ground in a heap of flailing limbs. Nicole managed to roll free and helped Paul pin the man's arms to the ground. Joey was lying across the man's legs, as if he'd fallen asleep there.

Suddenly the man freed one of his hands and grabbed Nicole by the ankle. Nicole screamed.

Jessica was on the other side of the clearing, holding Tanya in her arms. "There's rope in the cabin, Liz," she shouted.

Elizabeth ran inside and found a coil of rope on the floor. When she returned outside, Paul and Nicole had managed to pin the struggling man down again, each of them holding down one arm while Joey remained slumped across his knees.

Paul looked up, his face drenched with sweat. "Thanks," he said, gasping for breath as he took the rope from Elizabeth. "Just what we need."

When the madman was completely tied up, Elizabeth helped Joey to his feet. Jessica let Tanya go, and the girl went running into her brother's arms. Paul swept her up and hugged her tightly, a tear rolling down his face. Elizabeth's heart melted as her own tears fell.

Jessica had found the madman's discarded ax. She stood over him, gleefully holding the blade to his throat. "You shouldn't play with sharp objects," she taunted, her eyes filled with tears. Elizabeth cringed, imagining the horror her sister must have suffered.

Then Elizabeth glanced at Nicole. Without a word, they exchanged a hug. "You saved my life," Elizabeth cried. "You're so brave."

"I was never so scared in my life," Nicole said, sobbing.

Joey limped over to them. "Are you two all right?"

Nicole turned at him, her eyes flashing. "Yeah, Elizabeth and I are just great—except for the fact that we nearly lost our heads trying to save you. I can't believe you, Joey! Don't you know how stupid it was for you to come rushing up here by yourself? Thanks to you, we could have all been killed and—" Her voice broke on a sob. She took a deep, shaky breath and swallowed hard. "I'll never understand the macho mind," she said, shaking her head. She lifted her hands in a gesture of surrender. "I'm giving up, wonder twin.

You want him? You can have him. He's all yours."

Elizabeth watched her walk away, then turned to Joey with a questioning look.

"She's OK." He smiled softly. "I've known Nicole a long time. It's hard for her to step back from a fight, let alone apologize. Believe it or not, I think she just gave us her blessing."

Elizabeth wiped away her tears and stepped into his arms. Laying her head on his shoulder, she closed her eyes and allowed herself to relax. For the first time in weeks she felt safe.

"Listen," he whispered, his breath soft against her neck.

Elizabeth raised her head. She heard it, too—the whirring sound of a helicopter approaching. "Lights up," Paul said, and they all turned on their flashlights and waved them over their heads to signal their location.

The noise grew louder and louder, becoming deafening as a police helicopter landed in the clearing. Its bright lights illuminated the area so well that it seemed as if it were daytime. Four police officers jumped out, their guns drawn.

Minutes later the madman was taken away in handcuffs. When the helicopter had gone, the area seemed unusually dark and quiet. Everyone stood motionless, as if they all needed a moment to digest what had happened.

Tanya's voice broke the stillness. "Did we miss the s'mores at camp?"

Everyone laughed. Standing in the circle of Joey's arms, Elizabeth sighed with relief. The nightmare was finally over.

"I don't know what I'm going to do with you two," Paul teased as he and Jessica hiked back to camp, with Tanya riding on his shoulders.

A second helicopter had arrived at the clearing to pick up the group, but there hadn't been enough room for everyone to ride together. The pilot had offered to return for Paul and Jessica, but they'd declined his offer. Everyone had tried to persuade Tanya to get into the helicopter with Elizabeth, Joey, and Nicole, but she'd clung tearfully to Jessica and Paul and had adamantly refused to go without them.

Jessica held on to a low-hanging branch as she stepped across a shallow stream. "The question is, what are *we* going to do about *you?*"

Tanya giggled. "Why don't you guys just start kissing?"

Paul looked up at her and said with a pretend scowl, "What do you know about it, you little twerp?"

"I know Jessica is your girlfriend," she said. "And I know you're her boyfriend."

"Oh, do you now?" he said, clapping her feet together in front of him.

Tanya began to chant. "Paul and Jessica sitting in a tree, k-i-s-s-i-n-g . . ."

He turned to Jessica. "Should we dump her in that stream back there?"

"No way." Jessica giggled and reached up to clasp Tanya's hand. "This kid and I are true friends forever. And besides, Paul, we were up in a tree earlier this evening."

He laughed aloud. "Life was hard enough when I had only *this* crazy, stubborn girl to worry about," he said, jostling Tanya.

"Quit shaking me, or I'll throw up on your head," Tanya squealed. Jessica laughed.

Paul squeezed Jessica's hand. "If either of you girls ever pulls a stunt like this again . . ."

Jessica turned to him with a saucy grin. "Look who's talking about crazy stunts. What do you call crashing through a window, brandishing a pocket-knife?"

He grinned. "I call it saving the two prettiest necks in the whole world." He lifted her hand to his lips and kissed her palm.

"Oooo-ee! Kiss, kiss," Tanya cried.

Jessica smiled. A warm, peaceful feeling came over her. She was glad to be alive, to feel her heart brimming with joy. Deep inside, she knew that

Christian would have been happy for her, too.

The sun was just beginning to rise when they reached the camp, casting everything in a radiant pink light. A crowd was gathered outside the main lodge, and someone shouted, "They're here!"

Everyone cheered and clapped, giving Jessica, Paul, and Tanya a heroes' welcome. Elizabeth ran up to Jessica and hugged her tightly. Without words, volumes passed between them. She and Elizabeth shared a bond that stretched across any distance. When camp had first started, Jessica had worried that Elizabeth would be too preoccupied with Maria and writing to pay attention to her. Now Jessica realized how silly her fears had been. *Elizabeth will always be there for me,* she thought gratefully.

Tanya's fellow Wanna-bes mobbed her and Jessica, squealing and jumping joyfully. Maggie recorded the homecoming with her video camera. Finally the group began to file into the lodge.

As Jessica was about to follow Paul inside, Lacey grabbed her arm and pulled her aside. She fixed Jessica with a level stare. "You know the rules about boyfriends trespassing at Camp Echo Mountain."

With a sinking feeling, Jessica nodded.

"However, under the circumstances, I'm not even going to ask what Paul Mathis was doing in the woods," Lacey said. Then, to Jessica's surprise, she winked.

Lila awoke, stiff and sore, the side of her face pressed against a sharp rock. A damp chill penetrated her whole body, and she didn't know where she was. Her eyelids flew open in alarm. *Why am I lying in a ditch?* she wondered.

Then she remembered. She and Bo had come upon a gravel road in the forest sometime in the night and had followed it for miles without ever reaching civilization. Finally, having gotten to the point of exhaustion, they'd decided to camp for the night.

The scent of wet wool tickled her nostrils. She noticed that Bo's dark green shetland sweater was tucked around her shoulders. He must have covered her with it while she'd been sleeping. Propping herself up with her elbow, Lila lifted her head, groaning with pain.

Bo was sitting on the ground nearby, watching her. *I probably look like the star of a bad horror movie,* she thought.

"Good morning," he said, smiling brightly. "We survived the night."

Lila's expression softened. She had fallen asleep first, leaving him to face his fear of the woods all alone. "Oh, Bo, I know it couldn't have been easy for you."

He shrugged. "It wasn't too bad. I kept the fire

going and watched the stars—and you. Seeing the sunrise was neat, too."

"You weren't scared at all?" she asked.

"Yeah, I was. But knowing there wasn't anything I could do about it, I just let myself sit here and be scared." He shrugged. "After a while I got used to it."

"I think you're terrific," she said.

Bo stiffened suddenly. "Listen. Someone is coming."

Lila heard it, too—the sound of an approaching vehicle. Whooping and cheering, they ran to the road, prepared to flag down whoever it was. They were expecting a truck or a Jeep, but to their surprise, a small plane flew over their heads.

Dejected, Lila plopped down on the ground. "I don't suppose airplanes stop to pick up hitchhikers."

"This one does!" Bo shouted.

She looked up and gasped. Sure enough, the plane was landing a few hundred feet away, right in the middle of the road. Bo looked at her and laughed. Together they took off, running.

The gathering in the main lodge turned into a party. Spirits were high, and there was an all-you-can-eat buffet of peanut butter, sliced cheese, and frozen pizza—thanks to Winston, Derek, and Aaron, who had raided Bernard's kitchen.

Elizabeth was sitting with Maria and Nicole near the huge stone fireplace, where a deliciously warm fire crackled and glowed. "You can't believe how happy I am now that the two of you have finally become friends," Maria said.

Elizabeth squinted at Nicole. "Who, us? Are *we* friends?"

Nicole raised her eyebrows dramatically. "Gee, I don't know, wonder twin. Seems like a bizarre idea." They both burst out laughing.

"Friends or not, there's no one I'd rather face down an ax murderer with," Elizabeth declared.

Nicole smiled, the hint of a blush staining her cheeks. "Yeah, well . . . what can I say? Homicidal maniacs always bring out the best in me."

Maria hugged Elizabeth and Nicole around their necks. "It's a dream come true," she said, laughing.

"You're choking us, Maria," Nicole croaked jokingly.

Maria released them. Nicole made loud gagging noises, as if she'd been strangled. Elizabeth laughed and straightened the knotted sleeves of Joey's sweatshirt, which was draped around her shoulders. She hadn't planned on wearing it, but Nicole had made a point of saying that she wouldn't mind. Now Elizabeth was glad she had it, not so much for warmth as for the emotional comfort it gave her.

Jessica came over to them. "Have you guys seen Lila?" she asked. "I can't find her anywhere."

"Is Bo here?" Maria asked, scanning the room. "If you find him, I'm sure you'll find her."

"Have you been to the cabin?" Nicole asked.

Jessica shook her head. "No, why?"

Maria, Nicole, and Elizabeth looked at each other and laughed. "Lila was there," Elizabeth said. They had found some interesting changes in the cabin's decor when they'd gone to change into fresh clothes.

"Or at least her decorator was," Maria quipped.

Jessica frowned. "What's that supposed to mean?"

"You'll have to see for yourself," Maria replied.

Jessica shrugged. "I don't know about that girl. So, how's Joey's condition?" she asked Elizabeth. He had been taken to the first-aid cabin and was being watched by the camp nurse.

"The nurse said he was OK, but she hasn't let him leave her office yet." Elizabeth shuddered, remembering how pale he'd looked in the helicopter.

"Paul's parents are coming to pick up Tanya and take her to the doctor for a complete checkup. They were really shaken when Paul called them." Jessica smiled softly. "Tanya's not too happy about leaving camp early, poor kid. I'm going to go wait outside with her and Paul. If you see Lila, tell her I'm looking for her."

"Wait a minute, Jess," Elizabeth said. "You don't think something terrible might have happened to Lila and Bo, do you?"

"No, of course not," Jessica said. "Lila and Bo would never do anything risky. They've probably sneaked away to some fancy restaurant in town for a gourmet breakfast."

Maria laughed. "I can just see them now, trying to order caviar omelets and brioches in a cowboy diner."

Nicole looked over Elizabeth's shoulder and gestured with her chin. "Look who's here, wonder twin."

Elizabeth turned and saw Joey standing near the door. A feeling of relief came over her, as well as a flutter of excitement. "I have to go," she said.

Maria was staring at Nicole with a wary expression.

"Don't give me that look," Nicole told Maria. "For your information, I've decided Joey Mason isn't my type. I prefer blond guys. Like Derek, for instance."

Maria looked at her incredulously. "Since when?"

Nicole ignored the question, turning to Elizabeth. "I think Joey's waiting for you."

Maria threw her arms around Nicole and gave her a big hug.

"Oh, brother," Nicole muttered, rolling her eyes.

Elizabeth smiled, then hurried to Joey's side.

Chapter 15

Lila closed her eyes and murmured with delight as she savored the most delicious breakfast she'd ever eaten. She'd never imagined that a stale jelly doughnut could taste so marvelous.

She and Bo were standing in the middle of the road, leaning against the wing of the single-engine crop-dusting plane. Isaac Dollane, a commercial pilot from Billings, had been on his way north to spray wheat fields when he'd spotted them. After hearing their story, he had offered to give them a ride back to camp as soon as he cleared it with his boss.

Under different circumstances, Lila might have been apprehensive about climbing into a plane that wasn't much bigger than her Triumph convertible, especially with a pilot who looked more like the lead guitarist of a hard-core band. *This just happens to be one of those days when even a guy with tangled waist-length hair and a gold nose ring can look like a hero,* she thought.

Unfortunately, Isaac's half of the radio conversation didn't sound promising. "But it wouldn't take more than thirty minutes," he shouted into the mouthpiece.

When he was done, he turned to Lila and Bo and shrugged apologetically. "Sorry, guys. My boss has this thing about keeping on schedule."

Lila's heart sank. "Isn't there any way to change his mind?"

Isaac shook his head slowly. "The guy's impossible. Too bad this didn't happen a few months from now," he added. "We would've had the Dollane Brothers Company up and running by then. My brother and I are saving up to buy our own crop-dusting plane. We only need about another thousand or so."

"Let me get this straight," Bo said. "You only need another thousand dollars to buy a plane and start your own business?" There was a tinge of excitement in his voice.

Lila glanced at him curiously. "What are you getting at, Bo?"

"Think about it, Lila. A thousand dollars. That would only be five hundred each."

She raised her eyebrows. "We have no cash. Have you forgotten?"

"Yes, but we have plastic," he replied.

Lila snapped her fingers. "That's right. We can put it on our credit cards."

Isaac waved his hands, laughing. "Nice try, kids. But I've really got to get back to work, or I'll be out of a job. Lousy as it is, it still puts food on the table. I'll call the forestry service and let them know you're stranded out here."

"You don't think we're serious, do you?" Bo asked.

"You read my mind," Isaac said.

"Well, I never—" Lila muttered, incensed. "Bo, can you believe this guy? We're offering to invest in his business, and he's turning us down."

"Is it your pride?" Bo asked Isaac.

Isaac smiled indulgently. "No, it's not my pride. I'd be thrilled to let you invest in my business, but I don't believe either of you has that kind of money. We're talking about *a thousand dollars,* kids. Do you have any idea how much money that is?"

The insult stung, and Lila's temper flared. "Of all the nerve!" she said, raging. "I'll have you know I've got a dress back at camp that cost nearly twice that. And this—" She held up Bo's green sweater, which was now wrinkled and muddy. "This is a handmade sweater from the

Shetland Islands—part of the United Kingdom, if you didn't know. Do you have any idea what an authentic Shetland sweater costs?" She turned to Bo and saw him watching her with a look of admiration. Lila beamed proudly.

Isaac rubbed his hand across his chin. "Listen, if what you're saying is true . . ." He reached for the radio. "Hold on. I have to call my brother."

Lila and Bo held hands as they waited.

Isaac rolled his eyes as he spoke into the mouthpiece. "Yeah, yeah, yeah, I know you don't like to be bothered at work, but shut up and listen for a minute. This is an emergency." He explained the situation, and after a long pause, he said, "OK, I'll find out." He turned to Bo and Lila. "My brother wants to know if you have identification."

Bo reached for his wallet and whipped out his driver's license. Isaac took it from him and began to read the information over the radio. "Beauregard Creighton the third, Washington, D.C., license number zero four—" He frowned suddenly and asked, "What's so funny?"

After a pause, Isaac looked at Lila and asked, "Is your name Lila Fowler?"

"Yes, it is," she said, somewhat surprised.

He told his brother, listened for a moment, then let out a cheer. "We'll be there in ten minutes!" He ended the call and returned Bo's driver's license.

"My brother doesn't have to check you two out. He says he already knows you. So let's get going."

Bo and Lila exchanged curious looks as they climbed into the cockpit. "How does your brother know us?" Bo asked.

Isaac shrugged. "I have no idea. He only said that you're his best customers."

"But we've been stuck at camp for weeks," Lila countered. "Where does your brother work?"

Isaac slipped a set of headphones over his ears and replied, "Western Meadowlark."

Bo and Lila looked at each other and burst out laughing.

Elizabeth lost herself in the swirling passion of Joey's kiss. They had taken a leisurely walk along the shore of the lake, ending up in what Elizabeth considered to be their own special place—the woods behind the boathouse.

The kiss ended, and Elizabeth sighed contentedly. She felt as if all her senses had come to life, making her sharply aware of everything around her. The sun had risen and was shining warmly on her skin; the birds were singing sweetly in the trees.

"I just noticed you're wearing my sweatshirt," Joey said as he touched the loosely knotted sleeves hanging down from Elizabeth's neck.

"It's a nice sweatshirt," she said absently, gazing into his deep green eyes.

"It looks a lot better on you than it ever did on me," he said, studying her with an intent look. "You're so lovely, Elizabeth. Last night when I came to and saw you standing there—you were the most beautiful vision I'd ever seen."

Elizabeth gently touched the dark bruise on Joey's face. "I was so scared when you came stumbling out of the cabin," she said softly.

Joey chuckled, leaning back against the side of the boathouse. "I probably would've been scared, too—if I had known what was going on. The whole ordeal zipped right by me. One minute I was pounding on the door of the old cabin, and the next minute I was lying facedown in the dirt, across a pair of bony legs."

Elizabeth drew in a deep, shaky breath and wrapped her arms around his lean waist. "If we hadn't gotten there when we did, you might have been killed—"

"Hush," Joey whispered, softly rubbing her shoulders. "I'm fine now, really."

Elizabeth squeezed her eyes shut. A few hot tears spilled down her cheeks. *I almost lost him last night,* she thought, trembling. *And when camp ends, I'll lose him again.* Hundreds of bittersweet images flashed through her mind: listening to Joey tell ghost stories around the campfire . . . watching him direct the camp play . . . catching sight of him across the chaos of the mess hall . . . seeing him smile back at her . . . feeling the warmth of his arms around her as they canoed together over the cool water of Lake Vermillion. . . .

Elizabeth opened her eyes and gazed at him through the veil of her tears. "I can't believe I met you just a few short weeks ago," she murmured. "So much has happened."

Joey tenderly brushed away one of her tears with his thumb, then took hold of her hands, entwining his fingers with hers. "I could spend a lifetime getting to know all the fascinating things about you," he said.

Elizabeth swallowed against the painful lump in her throat. *A lifetime,* she thought, sadly realizing how little time they had left. A million emotions churned inside her. "Oh, Joey . . ."

She wanted to tell him so many things, but words seemed inadequate to express how much he meant to her, how alive with passion she felt when she was with him. Elizabeth pressed her lips against his and put her whole heart and all of her feelings into a deep, lingering kiss.

When their lips parted, they continued to hold each other close. Elizabeth rested her head on

Joey's shoulder and closed her eyes, memorizing the way it felt to be in his arms.

"I don't suppose there's a chance—" Joey whispered, stroking her forehead with his lips. Elizabeth looked up and saw a glimmer of hope in his eyes. "Is there any chance for us, Elizabeth?" he asked.

She lowered her eyes. With all her heart she wished there were, but she knew their relationship had reached its end.

"I guess that means no," Joey said.

"I'm so sorry," she said.

He smiled wistfully and pushed back a strand of hair that had escaped her ponytail. "Summer love . . . as fleeting as the light of a firefly."

It was a line from her play, but Elizabeth felt as if she were hearing it for the first time. The words had never before sounded so sad—and so hopeless.

"How can I say good-bye to you?" Joey groaned as he moved in for another searing kiss. Elizabeth closed her eyes, wondering the same thing. Suddenly a hazy image of Todd's face pushed its way into her mind, plunging her into a sea of confusion. *I love them both!* she thought, racked with guilt.

A few minutes later Elizabeth forced herself to do what she knew she must. She untied the sleeves of his Yale sweatshirt and shrugged it off her shoulders. A cascade of tears streamed down her face as she reverently folded the dark blue shirt and held it out to him. She knew there wouldn't be any hope for her relationship with Todd if she were to take Joey's sweatshirt home with her.

Joey looked stricken. "I want you to keep it, Elizabeth. That way you'll always have something to remember me by."

Elizabeth shook her head. "I can't. I don't—" She choked back her sobs and took a deep breath. "I don't need anything to help me remember you, Joey. You'll be in my heart forever."

He nodded grimly as he took the shirt. "I'll always remember you, too, Elizabeth," he said as he tied it around his waist.

Elizabeth wiped her hand across her wet cheek and closed her eyes. She still didn't know if she and Todd had a future. *Will I be able to stop loving Joey when I return to Sweet Valley?* she wondered.

Screaming, Lila squeezed her eyes shut and pressed her forehead into Bo's shoulder as the tiny airplane lifted off the ground. She, Bo, and Isaac were packed into the cockpit of the crop-dusting plane—which was a one-seater.

When she and Bo had first seen how small the

cockpit was, they had questioned the possibility of three people being able to fit inside it. Isaac had told them not to worry, that they would simply "prop open the doors." Lila and Bo had assumed it was a figure of speech, a technical term that pilots used.

Lila frantically kicked her feet, which were dangling from the plane into the open sky. Her screams were swallowed up by the roar of the engine and by the sound of the wind swirling through the open cockpit like a tornado.

It seems that "prop open the doors" is a term that lunatics use! she thought.

After Mr. and Mrs. Mathis had driven away with Tanya, Paul pulled Jessica into his arms. "Good morning," he whispered.

Jessica looked up into his gorgeous dark eyes and smiled. "Good morning yourself."

He lifted her hand to his lips and kissed it. "There are so many things I want to say to you, Jessica, but—"

She leaned closer and kissed him softly. "Me too."

By unspoken agreement, they leisurely wandered over to the main picnic table, hand in hand. The lake shimmered in the morning light, and the sky was decorated with fluffy white clouds.

Jessica and Paul climbed up on a picnic table and sat side by side, their feet braced on the seat. Jessica snuggled closer to him and took a deep breath of the cool, damp morning air. It had been a beautiful—and exciting—summer. Jessica couldn't believe camp was almost over—and with it, her romance with Paul. "I love this place," she said softly. "And I love you."

Paul gazed into her eyes for a long moment, then reached for her hand and entwined his fingers with hers. "I love you, too. Thank you for teaching me to trust again, Jessica."

She laid her head on his shoulder. "Oh, Paul, thank you for teaching me to love again, and for reminding me how great it feels to be alive." Closing her eyes, she rubbed her cheek against the soft fabric of his well-worn denim shirt.

Paul kissed Jessica's forehead, then pulled her into his arms for a deep, searing kiss that left her shaken.

Just then the sound of a motor filled the air, growing louder and louder. They looked at each other and frowned. The noise had also drawn a crowd from the main lodge. "What the—" Paul began.

Suddenly a small single-engine plane flew over the camp and circled above the main field. A pair of legs was hanging out of the open cockpit.

"Oh, gosh, I think those are Lila's shoes!" Jessica shouted.

She and Paul hopped down from the table and joined the others who were running toward the field. The plane landed and bounced across the grassy field until it came to a complete stop.

A gasp of astonishment rose from the crowd as Lila slid out of the plane, followed by Bo and another man. "We're home," Lila called out breathlessly.

Jessica gaped in shock at the incredible sight. Banging her pan and spoon, Lacey pushed her way through the group and began firing questions at Lila and Bo. "Where have you two been? Who is this man? And for Pete's sake, whose plane is this?"

Lila's face beamed with pride. "It's ours—or at least a small part of it anyway—and this is Issac Dollane, one of our partners. I believe Bo and I have just gone into the crop-dusting business."

"I can't believe you guys went out and helped buy an airplane," Maria said to Lila later that morning. The JCs had been given the day off to recuperate from the harrowing events of the previous night.

"I can't believe you flew back to camp with your legs dangling in the air," Jessica said.

194

Elizabeth looked around the cabin, marveling at all that had happened in just a few short weeks. *And it's about to end,* she thought sadly. *Everyone in this cabin has to say good-bye to someone special,* she realized. Nicole and Maria would be parting ways. Angela and Justin were no longer a couple. Elizabeth, Jessica, and Lila would be going back to Sweet Valley High without their summer loves.

"It was an exciting date," Lila said. "But I'm sure it can't compare to being tied up by an ax murderer. You win, Jess."

Jessica laughed and tossed her pillow at Lila. "Guess you'll have to try harder next time," Jessica said.

Lila tossed the pillow back but hit Angela instead. Angela threw the pillow at Lila. It brushed the top of Lila's head and landed on Maria's nightstand, knocking her tissue box to the floor.

After that, war broke out, with pillows whipping across the room and feathers flying everywhere.

Monday morning, before sunrise, Elizabeth gazed out over the dark, shimmering lake as she tried to sort out her jumbled feelings. *Camp is really over,* she realized. In four hours Darlene would be arriving to drive the California JCs to the airport in Billings, where an afternoon flight would take them home.

Elizabeth had come to her favorite place in the camp to think. But now, sitting on a tree stump in the woods behind the boathouse, she felt more confused than ever. It was as if a part of her and Joey's love had remained behind in this very spot, like the ghosts of Cassandra and the woodsman, the doomed lovers in *Lakeside Love*.

Tears welled up in Elizabeth's eyes. *I miss Joey so much, it's as if my heart were dying,* she thought. *But what about Todd?*

On Elizabeth's lap, her journal lay open to a blank page. She'd brought it along because writing about her problems usually helped her to see things more clearly.

Blinking away her tears, Elizabeth removed the cap of her pen and wrote "Todd" across the page in bold capital letters. Staring at his name, she recalled all the things she loved about him.

His friendly smile . . . his warm coffee brown eyes . . . Elizabeth took a deep, shaky breath and began to write. "Todd isn't afraid to admit when he's wrong. He's dependable, loyal, thoughtful, honest—"

A sudden noise startled her, and she froze, her pen poised over the page.

It was probably nothing, she thought as she slowly rose to her feet and nervously glanced around at the dark, shadowy woods that surrounded her.

I'm just feeling a bit edgy because I'm so upset. I'm going to have to learn to relax and—

Then she heard it again—the distinct clop of an ax chopping wood.

Choking back a scream, Elizabeth turned and ran.

Don't miss the next two Sweet Valley High Magnas, **Jessica's Secret Diary, Volume II,** *and* **Elizabeth's Secret Diary, Volume II.** *Find out about Elizabeth's painful decision and Jessica's devious romance, featuring classic moments from Sweet Valley High books #40-#70! The twins' secrets have never been jucier!*

Then, a new guy moves to town, and Jessica feels an attraction so strong, it's almost supernatural! Read all about it in Sweet Valley High #126, **Tall, Dark, and Deadly,** *book one in a chilling three-part miniseries. Experience the horror lurking in the dark shadows of Sweet Valley!*

Bantam Books in the Sweet Valley High series
Ask your bookseller for the books you have missed

SIGN UP FOR THE SWEET VALLEY HIGH® FAN CLUB!

Hey, girls! Get all the gossip on Sweet Valley High's® most popular teenagers when you join our fantastic Fan Club! As a member, you'll get all of this really cool stuff:

- Membership Card with your own personal Fan Club ID number
- A Sweet Valley High® Secret Treasure Box
- Sweet Valley High® Stationery
- Official Fan Club Pencil (for secret note writing!)
- Three Bookmarks
- A "Members Only" Door Hanger
- Two Skeins of J. & P. Coats® Embroidery Floss with flower barrette instruction leaflet
- Two editions of *The Oracle* newsletter
- Plus exclusive Sweet Valley High® product offers, special savings, contests, and much more!

Be the first to find out what Jessica & Elizabeth Wakefield are up to by joining the Sweet Valley High® Fan Club for the one-year membership fee of only $6.25 each for U.S. residents, $8.25 for Canadian residents (U.S. currency). Includes shipping & handling.

Send a check or money order (do not send cash) made payable to "Sweet Valley High® Fan Club" along with this form to:

SWEET VALLEY HIGH® FAN CLUB, BOX 3919-B, SCHAUMBURG, IL 60168-3919

NAME_____
(Please print clearly)

ADDRESS_____

CITY_____ STATE _____ ZIP_____
(Required)

AGE_____ BIRTHDAY_____ /_____ /_____